John Williams

Wordsmith

Preface by Keith Ely

Compiled by Lynda Roughley

IBSN 0 9518573 0 4 Wordsmith. (Pbk).

Published by Lynda Roughley Enterprises 1991

Cover photograph by John Davidson

Cover design by Martin Kelly

Printed by Scotprint (North West) Limited

Contents:

For John

who marched to the beat of a different drummer

Acknowledgements

With grateful thanks to all who helped in so many ways with the compilation of this book.

Particularly Linda, Keith, Graham and Martin.

About John Williams

John Williams? Ah, well, yes. How shall I put this? He was a bit of a prickly character, with a mysterious sense of humour. No, let's try that again. He was a colleague, well, at times he felt like a friend . . . but with a fiercely barbed wit that could make you feel like his enemy.

No, that's not quite it either. John was never going to be that easy to pigeon-hole. Behind those eyes, deep-set in a round, ruddy, bearded face, there were incredible depths - of intelligence, of humour, of mischief, of sadness.

From a distance, he was renowned for his loud, boisterous manner generally employed to embarrassing effect not only in bars but also, if he spotted the opportunity, in the office. In particular, he seemed to enjoy roaring with laughter to the point where everyone around wished he would shut up. He knew that and simply did it all the more.

Those who were closer knew him differently. He was a brilliant raconteur, a charming host, a notorious flirt, a proud father . . . and a late convert to the joy of tenorissimo arias. He fought years of illness and finally succumbed just when we thought he was going to achieve another miraculous recovery.

I met him 20 years ago when we worked together on the newsdesk of the *Liverpool Daily Post & Echo.* He hated the job and managed to convey the idea that he was only doing it as a favour to the boss. He loathed the intense pace of news gathering, he resented the need to be polite to the succession of mundane or abusive callers and he all but cried at the sheer predictability of the routine.

For John was a writer, not an organiser. More than that, he was a craftsman of our language and when, in the brief interludes between those newsdesk 'phone calls, we spoke, he dwarfed me with his mastery of words, always so carefully chosen, so precise in conveying his thoughts and ideas.

It was inevitable that he would gravitate towards a job where he could exercise this talent to the full and in so doing he has left us with a cache of brilliant, witty features that suggest him as perhaps the most distinguished columnist the *Daily Post* ever had.

Of course, he was vain about his writing abilities. With just cause. And he resented anyone either feeding him with an idea or trying to get him to write anything beyond his two famous weekly features - his Wednesday column and his TV review, into which he channelled all of his creative energy. (Well, nearly all, he would have said, with a crafty wink towards his children.)

And like all great writers he was given to extraordinary swings of temperament. He was angry on the occasions he struggled to find the words he needed, sulky when his columns failed to take the shape he had imagined, and intensely happy when it all came out right.

Mostly it did come out right. And for a very good reason. When John Williams wrote, he always chose the subject he knew best - himself. All of his columns were intensely personal, charged with his own emotion and frequently bristling with controversy. Whether he was railing at cab drivers (who subsequently threatened to boycott the *Daily Post*), surgery receptionists or football fans, John wrote with passion.

That passion seemed still to be simmering behind his eyes when last I saw him at Arrowe Park Hospital, Birkenhead, a couple of days before he died. He was struggling to pull off another recovery and spoke about returning home soon.

I egged him on, asking if he had any idea when he expected to be back at work. That night he told another visitor: "Here I am at death's door and all the bloody editor can do is worry about when I'm coming back to work."

We would all have wished to see that day.

We have, as consolation, this marvellous selection of his *Daily Post* columns. They cover the later years of his writing and encompass a tremendous breadth of subject. But all have that common thread - the wry perspective of a gifted writer who could make you laugh and wince within the space of a single, precision-turned paragraph.

Keith Ely,

Editor, ***Daily Post***

CHIPS AND OTHER DELICACIES

ALTHOUGH always the joker in the pack, John felt seriously about many issues and was prepared to stand up and be counted, regardless of how unpopular that might make him.

His views were always carefully reasoned and few issues escaped his pen, which was sometimes dipped in acid - particularly when writing about bureaucracy. He could not abide cant and twaddle and loved to poke fun at anyone full of their own self-importance.

Humorous writing is an extremely difficult craft but with his unique sense of fun and talent he mastered it and used it to full advantage. Whether writing about serious or light matters he was able to bring a smile to the face - and that was always his aim.

19 April, 1989

The chips are down for our national dish

THURSDAY is special. It's Brownies night and it's dancing night, which means that peace reigns in the house until 6.45 here. I am not at all sure what heaven is like, but this must be an ecstatic approximation.

One child is engaged in tying Brown Owl in knots while the other aspires to being the world's heaviest ballerina. Just keep away from our kitchen when she has her taps on. The discordant attempt at syncopation is sheer hell.

The day is also special because it is the lone occasion in the week when the kids are allowed chips. Returning from their exertions at what for them is a late hour, they have made a call at the "chippy" a mandatory excursion.

If I'm dreadfully unlucky, I get to share in the mess masquerading as fish, pies, mushy peas and lifeless slivers of what used to be potatoes. Really speaking, we should all wear black to mark the sad passing of the chip.

It died years ago when great and skilled practitioners in the art of frying shards of spud in bubbling beef dripping sold out. To make a fast buck, they sacrificed a noble tradition on the altar of Mammon.

Admittedly, there is still Harry Ramsden's place in Yorkshire, but it is hardly just around the corner for those of us domiciled in the red brick suburbia of Wallasey and its environs.

I find it strange, not to say antisocial, that the Monopolies Commission never investigated the obvious conspiracy that led to chippies being taken over by ... well, not to put too fine a point on it, foreigners.

It's not that I object to their nationalities or that I am consumed by xenophobia but, dammit all, the chip is peculiarly British. It has no historical place in the culture of those who now attract our custom with green neon tubes in their frontages.

I mean, did the Ming Dynasty flower and blossom on plates full of artery-hardening starch? Of course not. They were more interested in the crockery than what was on it.

Did any of the Caesars, between libidinous bouts of boozing, incest and making love to their horses, ever sprinkle salt and vinegar over piping hot serried ranks of solanum tuberosum? No. They were more interested in fiddling while watching bonfires on a grand scale.

The Greeks were absorbed by Olympian and healthy pursuits or else creating philosophies on the lower slopes of Parnassus. The vital importance of a good chip completely eluded them.

Still, it did not prevent any of these disparate races taking over branches of a national institution and making a complete balls of the operation. They came, they saw and the chip uttered a tired gasp and was conquered. Maybe I should have said conkered.

Today's chip is repellent. It almost invites you to laugh at it or, in extremis, to be spiteful. It's colour is as inviting as a sick note and it sags in the middle like a geriatric who has just accomplished one-and-a-half push ups.

The taste is redolent of wet Polyfilla which cannot be disguised by a discreet dusting of salt and judicious drip of vinegar. As a window sealant they would be adequate, but only on a temporary basis.

Let there be no mistake. We are here debating a matter of national importance. Proper chips are what your mother used to make (assuming she could cook in the first place) and hit the palate like a lover with a detailed knowledge of erogenous zones.

They were always golden brown and cut to almost uniform length, held in tremulous fingers they would proudly stand up and be ready to be counted. There was always a pointed end with which to spear the yoke of an egg.

Indeed, so uniform were they that you could get at least seven to lie on a bed of bread and butter before folding it and salivating over the melting butter oozing from its crease. Rather generously we Brits gave the world the chip buttie.

In return, the world gave us fryers who have no respect for, or understanding of, the rightful place in society of the chip. To them it is merely an incidental accompaniment to pasta or noodles with fried rice.

My wife resolutely refuses to make them on the spurious grounds that she has jealously to guard her reputation as the best cook in the house. No-one is challenging her claim, but every Thursday she buys a newspaper full of those cotton wool imitations.

They are vile and soggy and properly belong in one of those laughable Tate Gallery still life exhibitions. Given the gullibility of those in charge, the pile of bricks could easily become the heap of dead chips.

It is a sign of the times that the only person I know who can make a decent chip is a Greek Cypriot by the name of Andreas Antoni. He had the savvy to dig deep into the British psyche and come up with a perfect answer - the tuberous torpedo of exactly the right colour.

But he is alone among those aliens like Mr Wang, who can perform wonders with what a friend describes as "green curry" and Mr Santi whose batter is sheer poetry, but who are consistently defeated by the chip.

It always emerges from their vats of fat wan and limp, as if in need of some sunshine or a brace of crutches. They could never pass the test of being held at one extremity and standing as erect as a guardsman.

A British institution is all but dead. What we need is a revolution with Lancastrians and Yorkshiremen buying out the Chinese, the Italians and the Greeks. It's the only way to make the chip respectable again.

7 August, 1984

Thoughts of little account

WITH THE sort of unfeeling cheerfulness which properly deserved a kick up the mailbag, the postman thrust a long white envelope into my tremulous hand. "Looks like one of those nasty ones," he said.

He was away too quickly to hear the wild rushing of blood in my ears or to notice the bodily reaction which had poured cement into my knee joints. There it was, that dreaded word - Private - set in bold type.

No need to wonder about the identity of the sender. No need to speculate about the contents. Obviously the £10 win on Spotting the Ball had been insufficient to avert the monthly disaster.

After what seemed like a fortnight some feeling returned to my legs and I limped into the kitchen, silently handing the gloom-laden missive to the chef. "I've been expecting that," she said with the dazzling smile of someone who had just received a birthday card instead of a terse warning from the bank.

With a panache more affected than felt, she quickly read it and dispatched it into the welcoming jaws of the bin. "Stupid computer. It should have known our salaries are being paid in tomorrow," she said.

To be reluctantly fair to the all-too vigilant computer, it had not been apprised of the fact that the salaries boasted of had already been accounted for by a glut of quarterly bills.

Bills of such enormity that the only realistic alternatives would seem to be cooking on a primus stove, illuminating the house with candles and eating copious amount of Mint Imperials to keep warm in the winter.

Having had some close encounters of the uncomfortable kind with the author of the letter, I immediately sank into a black depression. Banks can seriously damage your health.

There is only one thing a man can do in this situation. Summon up the gall to persuade his wife to accept the invitation to call in for a summit meeting with the manager.

At our last meeting I assured him that the situation would improve enormously when my wife returned to work after having the baby. "If we can't manage then, we need shooting," I said rashly. My logic is that he is less likely to point a gun at a woman.

Research in the office revealed that mail from the temples of Mammon affects colleagues in different ways. Some experience the beating of drums on the stomach lining while for others the sensation is one of nausea.

One, like me, is physically unable to open the envelope and another suffers acute depression before going out to buy some extravagance in a glorious act of defiance. Another lets successive letters lie unopened until the envelopes take on a legal look.

I found it perversely encouraging to discover that a journalist who is an absolute whiz at business and commerce handles his own affairs with all the expertise of a sozzled chimpanzee. It makes this fiscal nincompoop feel so much better.

Of course, it's not just the letters which strike terror in the heart. There's the risky business of actually entering the bank, raincoat collar pulled up on even the hottest day to avoid being recognised.

Then comes the fear-charged moment when the teller glances at your optimistic cheque and consults his black-list. You know instinctively that all is lost the moment he inquires, "Are you expecting any payments into your account?"

This is all part of the bank's strategy to reverse the natural order of things. To persuade you to give them money instead of the other way around. Your worst fears are realised if he walks away then returns to say that Mr so-and-so would like a word.

There are two choices. You can either stalk out in feigned high dudgeon or come face to face with someone who looks as if he is probably unplugged from a socket at 5.30 each evening.

It's rather like being called to the head's study to be chastised for not doing one's homework. And like any schoolboy you mumble apologies and promise to be good.

He, with his low interest overdraft and mortgage, cannot understand how you could be so irresponsible. You give an assurance that you will cut out such luxuries as food, soap and toilet paper.

On the strength of this, you are allowed to return shamefaced to the teller and collect a pitiful handful of notes. Now you can afford to drive through the Mersey Tunnel and buy a bag of crisps for Sunday lunch.

The likelihood is that you will also buy half a bottle of Scotch to blot out the trauma and to fire dreams of winning the Pools.

Not that it would make much difference. Years of playing the red letter game condition one. You could walk into the bank with a cheque for £1 million and still feel like a rabbit in a vivisection lab.

If my bank manager is reading this, I want him to know that I think he's marvellous and that his letters make me feel wanted. I just wish he didn't want me so often.

12 October, 1988

And lo, the meek shall be disinherited

THERE ARE some people who, bored with the familiar routines of life, seek elements of danger to experience a magical surge of adrenalin. They climb precipitous mountains, dive 100 feet into a damp face cloth or wrestle with mighty jawed reptiles in the Mersey.

Others, preferring a peaceful existence, sometimes have bizarre and unwanted hazards thrust upon them. These can often begin with your average, warm-hearted threatening letter from the Gas Board.

Couched in terms which could be absolutely ruinous for one's underwear, they are dispatched by faceless, nameless creatures who are imbued with religious zeal for the infallibility of their god - the computer.

Once it has spoken, its disciples, now armed with a dangerous array of Biros instead of swords of burning gold, must go forth and spread the word. And, yea, in the beginning that word was usually "Unless".

Ted Reynolds, a Liverpool insurance broker, had one of these theological encounters of the thoroughly unpleasant kind. The first tablet of stone pointed out that not only did he owe a lot of money, but he had prevented the black-clad Angels of Menace from reading his meter.

Being an amiable chap and wanting to placate the deity, Mr Reynolds telephoned to explain his situation. He was assured by an answering acolyte that he need worry no longer and would surely be forgiven.

But Computer God was not a merciful one and, in quick succession, the luckless sinner was smited with two more heavy tablets which threatened pestilence and famine in his home. Once more, Mr Reynolds picked up BT's instrument of confession and was granted absolution.

The acolyte asked to whom he had previously spoken. Resorting to words which had no biblical connotations, our Ted saith: "How the bloody hell do I know? You'll never tell me your names. What's yours by the way?" And the acolyte demurred, saying that the body divine would not allow such information to be divulged.

Anyway, probably fearing that he was in danger of losing a convert, the wrathful Computer God sent the biggest tablet of stone in his armoury - a proclamation that the bailiffs were on the way to smash down the door and read, and perhaps remove, the gas meter.

And Ted rejoiced and was exceeding pleased. From the warmth of his all-electric flat which has no gas meter, he told the Gas Board: "Do what the hell you like, and I'll sue you for every last penny I can squeeze from the courts."

And lo, Computer God went miraculously silent as some slow-thinking clod finally got the message and anointed it with the correct information.

The moral of this little parable is clear and serves to illustrate how inefficient and remote such bodies are capable of being. Perhaps it is because they have little incentive to be otherwise.

Such businesses that had to contend with competition from rivals would soon disappear down the tubes were they to adopt the same high-handed and snotty-nosed attitudes. Not that all smaller concerns are so marvellous, either.

You can count on very few fingers those shops and stores in which the staff are polite and are willing to serve without heaving an irritated sigh because you have unreasonably interrupted a conversation with a workmate.

However, to revert to the original point, far too much reliance is placed on computers in business. Whatever they spew out is accepted as gospel with no thought for the fact that whoever programmed it might have fingers like bananas and have mistyped the information.

It is a measure of the Gas Board's remoteness from the public that, even after all his protestations, not one nameless member of staff thought to check the authenticity of his claims. They just relentessly pursued their campaign of rude threats. And all because a machine told them so.

22 October, 1986

Justice? More a way of life!

THE YOUNG man had got himself hopelessly drunk, impulsively acquired a chunk of meat for which he neglected to pay and then got himself nicked. Now he stood in the dock, a bowed, sullen figure, awaiting his fate.

The magistrates - a matching set of three - conferred in whispers and the one with the speaking role announced a fine of £50. The defendant reacted as if someone had just attached electrodes to his sensitive bits.

"Fifty quid?" he yelped. "I t'ink dat's too bloody much."

Clearly taken aback by this irreverent attempt at barter the JP said rather lamely, "We're not here to argue with you." The clerk then arranged the HP-like terms on which the miscreant would pay his debt to justice.

Next up were two teenage lasses who had devised their own economical system of enhancing their wardrobes. They pleaded guilty to shoplifting, the prosecutor did his bit and the girls - dressed up to the threes - were invited to say something in mitigation.

They declined even to feign regret for their youth opportunities project and accepted their penalties without expression. Before they reached the doors of No.3 court, cigarettes were already between scarlet lips and a fit of giggles under way.

No.3 is one of 16 courts presided over by Liverpool City Magistrates. Such are the frailties of the populace that barring Sundays, there is only one day a year when they do not operate - the one marking the birth of Christ.

For the defendants, whatever their religious persuasion God is temporarily the usually middle-class, middle-aged guy on the Bench with the awesome power to alter their lives. Lots of prayers are silently offered up in this building.

"You'll get nothing in No.3," an usher told me. "That's the rubbish court." This was a reference to the pettiness of the offences rather than the quality of life clearly not enjoyed by those arraigned there.

There are always a handful of D and Is (drunk and incapables) awaiting their moments of truth, but they don't seem aware of it. They sit at the back of the court empty-eyed, staring into space or else sending index fingers on exploratory forays up their nostrils.

Some had probably spent the night on those hard wooden beds in the Bridewell, the ones steeply pitched so that in moments of sickness the vomit will slide down the incline rather than back down the throat of the regurgitator.

For the habitual drunk it's all a matter of routine. A fine of £5 or one day, which means just sitting around until the court recesses. Then it's a reunion with bottles of competitively priced plonk from far-flung outposts of the Commonwealth.

Outside is the rectangle, like the chilly-tiled waiting room of a Victorian hospital, where Liverpool's Les Miserables listen for the traumatic moment when their names are bawled out, bouncing off the high ceiling and into the surrounding courts.

In their midst is a large woman with ravaged features, fish-netted thighs straining against a mini-skirt that would have looked pathetic even on someone 35 years younger. I'm told it used to take three policemen to subdue her in the old days. Now she's on the wagon, but still likes to pay social visits to No.3.

I was there one day when the magistrate spotted her and, just like an old mate, called out, "What are you doing here, Catherine?" "I've been missing you, sir," she replied with the naughtiest of twinkles in her eye.

In No.2 solicitor Paul Rooney, tall and good-looking in an angular sort of way, successfully gets bail for a small-time drug user. His two co-defendants, allegedly major league pedlars, shake his hand before being returned to the misery of Risley.

A good start to Mr Rooney's working day, then he has to explain why his next client is not present. He is said to have impersonated a police officer while out on bail and is again enjoying the remand centre's hospitality. Some people never learn.

The next case involves yet another Rooney client but she too, fails to appear. "She usually comes, but she tends to be late," her advocate explains. The court is not amused and there is talk of issuing a warrant. Jenny Come-Lately might regret this day.

Beneath the court a heavy door slams each time a prisoner is brought up from the Bridewell cells. As they emerge, they invariably look not at the Bench but to the back of the court, hoping for an encouraging smile and wave from wives and girlfriends.

They are flanked by heavy men of HM Prisons. Such is the grinding process of law that this contact with the outside world will be all too brief. Dates for committal proceedings are set and in just a couple of minutes they are on their way back to the cells.

The door below is slammed behind them and in their troubled minds it must sound like the crack of doom. It could be months before they go for trial. Innocent until proven guilty, but locked away all the same. Just the thought gives me the shudders.

In the waiting room the big woman is sharing her experiences with anyone who will listen and dispensing expert advice. She reckons she can tell to the penny how much they are likely to be fined, then she cadges some pennies from a passing reporter. They are on first-name terms, veterans of the court both.

It is lunchtime and the other veterans - the D and Is - are free to crawl back inside their bottles of bad dreams. But they'll be back. Lots of people come back. Only they and God know why.

The big woman heads for the street with the rest of us. She too, will return. For some, being in court is a way of life.

10 December, 1986

Hygiene: The nail varnished truth

DEVILLED, coddled, poached, boiled, scrambled or fried, I love eggs in all their cholesterol glory. All those dieticians can go suck their thumbs. When it comes to ovum I adore 'em.

Except, that is, when one has a nail-varnished finger poked into it. I'm funny that way. It goes heavily against the grain to see a foreign digit, which has been goodness knows where else, being carelessly inserted into one's breakfast.

It's a meal I rarely eat, but when the urge takes me I slip over to a cafe near the office for a toasted egg and bacon sandwich. Or, at least, I did until encountering a girl whose apparent concept of hygiene is not to juggle with pig slurry while simultaneously serving butties.

A waitress bearing the delicacy was en route to my table when she was accosted by Miss Clean, who wondered if the sandwich was for one of her customers. With all the academic subtlety of Sherlock Holmes she stuck her index finger under the "lid" to ascertain the contents.

It was then presented to me, now bristling like a baited badger with a hangover. I made a dignified complaint and the waitress turned the colour of a marigold. "How else d'yer expect 'er to find out what was innit?" she demanded.

Rather timorously, because by now all the staff and customers were listening in, I suggested she might have used tongs. Judging by her expression, I might just have well suggested she read War and Peace between tea breaks.

"Oh sorry, very sorry," she said with sarcasm heavier than a battleship. "I'll take it back to the kitchen." She did, but there is no doubt in my mind that the egg I consumed was exactly the same one that was subjected to the Revlon-coated talon test.

That was bad enough. Even worse was the atmosphere which was only marginally warmer than an Eskimo's hooter. The staff shot me glances laced with venom and the clientele looked at me with undisguised suspicion. How very British of me then to start feeling guilty.

I slunk back to the office and wrote a letter to the proprietor. His reply was firmly based on the principle that not only is the customer always wrong, he is also a bloody nuisance. In effect, he was saying that they were far too busy to be bothered with the piffling business of hygiene.

His attitude seemed to be that the finger was an optional extra and I should be grateful it came free of charge. My complaint had obviously not wrought drastic changes in his kitchen.

Days later I was in a pub watching the barman, properly using tongs, loading up a display case with sandwiches and rolls. Perhaps the previous night's intake of ale got to him because his hand suddenly quivered and a big cheese and onion batch ended up in the sink used to wash glasses.

With some dexterity he employed the tongs to retrieve it - then carefully placed it alongside the others, impervious to the fact that some poor sucker was likely to ingest a mouthful of Cheddar garnished with Fairy Liquid. To my eternal shame I said nothing.

There's nothing more damaging to one's image than being thrown out of a boozer for being a trouble-maker. Besides, it was interesting to hang around and see if anyone oozing pale green foam from the mouth made a sudden dash for the toilet.

In one of those posh country restaurants (the sort which charges a viewing fee for letting you look at the menu) I found a metal nut in my starter. "Ah, we've been wondering where that got to," said the delighted maitre d' hotel neglecting to inquire after the state of my teeth. With overwhelming largesse he knocked 50 pence off the bill.

I finally came to the conclusion that our national attitude to catering hygiene is less than serious and carried out a brief survey among friends. Talk about instant botulism. It's a wonder they've not been hospitalised.

The worst story came from a pal who went to his office canteen to order a ham sandwich. When it arrived the bread was stained in such a way that he at first thought someone had mistakenly added red cabbage to the filling.

"Sorry about that," said the unperturbed assistant. "The chef's cut his finger."

A colleague recounted the horror of seeing a squad of greenfly marching up his knife when he disturbed a salad. On turning over the lettuce he found a whole battalion had set up camp. The greenery was whisked away and brought back by the manageress.

She could see nothing wrong with it, she said. The crafty minx. She had evicted the top tier of squatters, but had left in residence those still lurking on the underside of the cos. She was forced to concede she had brought back the original meal.

A voluptuous woman of my acquaintance decided to go on a quite unnecessary diet and took to buying portions of ready-roasted chicken. Imagine her delight when she discovered blood oozing from one piece and a sheaf of singed feathers concealed under the wing.

She all but gagged. Back at the shop a cheery sales assistant inquired, "Did we charge you extra for the feathers?" in sheer indifference to the customer's well-being.

There were scores of other horror stories and you can only despair that no-one seems to give a damn as long as they are making a fast quid. I have never been back to the egg-and-bacon cafe. They gave me one finger so, with characteristic generosity, I have given them two.

17 December, 1986

Wine, snake and quips

I THINK it was John Mortimer who said that if you know a writer, sooner or later you'll end up appearing in his columns. It's so true. I have to admit I cannot talk to friends without keeping a professional ear cocked for a good tale.

The dinner table is an excellent listening post, even before the wine has performed its dirty trick of prising indiscretions from minds freed of normal restraints. Once uncorked, it emits the blended bouquets of hilarity, mental stimuli, mild rudery and little daggers of character assassination.

The food becomes almost incidental as you digest the mixture of personalities and wonder if the conversation might take on a slightly fraught air, if the jokes will be too risque or if Tory and Socialist might clash over the cabinet pudding.

It's the most satisfying form of entertainment I know, a bit of pure theatre in your own - or someone else's - home. For two or three hours you have a room alive with a richness of words meant to amuse, to engage, provoke, tease and, sometimes to taunt. I love it

One of my recent guests convulsed me with a story about his brother, who used to be a vet dealing with mainly domestic pets. Since Merseyside cannot be described as even sub-tropical he was slightly thrown when a client brought in a snake.

It seemed the pet had carelessly slithered over a piece of glass and cut its belly. Getting out his snake book, or whatever the appropriate manual was, the vet gave himself a crash course in reptile surgery and stuck the snake in the fridge to get it's body temperature right for the op.

He forgot about it for a while and it came out almost as rigid as a walking stick. Later, he sewed up the gash, charged the client £30 and sent him on his way rejoicing. But not for long.

He returned two days later complaining that the snake was in obvious discomfort and that its body was badly distended. Our friend consulted his book again, this time in more detail, and was horror struck to discover that he had actually sewn up the poor creature's bottom.

Our talk turned from the living to the dead, namely that vastly boring advertising campaign for the sale of British Gas and the mysterious, but eventually irritating, Sid. It was as if we had waved a red rag at one of the women present.

She recounted in uproarious details how, over the space of several months, she had battled with BG to have a gas fire properly repaired. First they fixed a simple fault, but somehow contrived to knock off the water heating system.

It was the start of an unfunny saga which became a farce culminating in her having no fire, no boiler and a flood of muddy water in the morning room. Four engineers looked with mild interest at the damage they had done and decided to beat a retreat.

My friend was enraged. Months of pent-up anger welled up inside her, so she actually locked the men in the room and told them they would not be leaving until the mess had been tidied up. The key went inside her bra, she poured a stiff brandy and, as an afterthought, bellowed through the door. "If you see Sid, tell him I'll castrate him."

While she is something of a spitfire when her dander is up, her husband tends to be a gentle soul willing to believe the best of everyone. Even the criminals with whom he deals in the course of his job. At times I despair of him.

He recounted how their home had been burgled no fewer than ten times. No matter how many times they changed the locks, the thieves always found a way in. The front door came to look like a little corner of Alcatraz, so the "visitors" simply removed it from its hinges.

He lost four video recorders, a collection of musical instruments, jewellery, antiques and his great grandfather's Franco-Russian War medals, which were of great sentimental value. You would think his view of the world would have been a little jaundiced.

His home was ransacked for the tenth time only three weeks ago and his prized collection of wood-carving tools stolen. "I was very angry at the time," he told us, "but I don't mind too much if they've been nicked by someone who likes carving and otherwise couldn't afford them." I could have smacked his soppy legs.

Anyway, it was a good dinner and the subject of eating prompts me to hark back to last week's column about catering hygiene. It struck a chord with Keith Tyler, of Bangor, who remembers vividly buying a salad roll to eat at his desk while he worked.

"Taking my usual enormous bites, I did notice the roll was more gritty than usual," he writes. "Then I heard something drop from it on to my desk top. I was horrified to see half a juicy earthworm wriggling in pain, presumably because its head end was on its way to my stomach.

"Not wanting to make a spectacle of myself I refused to pass out, settling instead for a change of deathly white pallor to a beautiful emerald green. My colleagues reacted in similar manner. No words were said, but they all stopped eating their rolls.

"The public health inspector said my worm was not admissible as evidence because it died the next day and, for the sake of evidence it had to be alive on the day of court appearance. So whenever you order a salad roll always check the contents, as you may destroy the evidence."

Thank you Mr Tyler, I'm sure your tale has ruined many a breakfast this morning, but it was a story which deserved telling. It just goes to show that even eating your greens like a good boy can be very bad for you.

3 August, 1988

Talking of rubbish ... brings me to councillors

I CAN ALWAYS tell when the refuse collectors have called. You don't have to belong to the CID to follow the trail of litter out of the street, which is where my empty bins are always left.

It's all right having the flash to be a two-bin family, but how much flashier to have collectors who recognise one's prestige in society by bringing the damn things back.

I expect it's something to do with a great efficiency scheme dreamed up by a councillor who is even now recovering from a full frontal lobotomy. They all suffer from delusions of adequacy.

Incapable of organising naughtiness in a bawdy house, you should see the impact they make on the international community. How Pretoria must have trembled when Wirral Borough Council threatened to rename Hamilton Square after Nelson Mandela.

Nelson's name does not often crop up in Birkenhead's ale houses. The more politically aware topers probably think he is a wrestling hold invented by Kent Walton.

In any case, they are probably labouring under another misapprehension: namely, that they voted for councillors who would look after their interests rather than exercise their mighty insolence in world affairs.

Why bother about bins when you can waste time making futile empty gestures? Why consider the wishes of the electorate when you can indulge yourself as a practising idiot at the ratepayers' expense?

Mandela is the magnificently obdurate victim of a regime which has no moral right to exist. Unfortunately, he is also an implacable advocate of violence and murder, so making Pretoria his prisoner as much as he is theirs.

Only recently his chief disciple, Winnie, gloated: "We still have our matches and our tyres." This was a chilling reference to the barbaric practice of draping a petrol-soaked tyre around someone's neck and setting fire to it.

Does Birkenhead really deserve a square named after a man who condones this horrific form of death? Why not dedicate the place to a thug of the IRA, whose cause is arguably as just but whose methods are equally repellent?

The trouble with party politics is that it allows you to gorge yourself on ideology whilst starving yourself of integrity.

Did you ever meet a councillor who didn't claim he was a servant of the public, merely carrying out the wishes of those who voted him into power? And did you ever encounter one who didn't march into the chamber and bravely - if robotically - adhere to party dogma whatever the best interests of the electorate?

But, to give credit where it is due, it is true to say that many of our burghers are honest-to-goodness hypocrites - right up to the point where they verge on being silly burghers. (I've waited years to use that phrase.)

What would you make of those Wirral councillors who gave their children a private education and now seek to abolish the borough's best grammar schools? Slaves to the party line, or merely hypocrites and traitors?

I know a raving anti-Thatcherite headmaster, who stuffs comprehensives down your gullet with little prompting. But what is good for your children wasn't good enough for his. He sent them to fee-paying schools.

Double standards apply at all levels of politics. Like Neil Kinnock touring the front-line African states and preaching the virtues of sanctions against South Africa.

Then he sat down to a meal at which Cape wine was served. Some sanction. "That was a question worthy of 'The Sun'," was his feeble response when an observant reporter pointed out what he was doing.

What he was doing was being human, which often conflicts with the noises which emanate from the silver-coated mouths of politicians. It's a classic case of "do as I say" rather than "do as I do."

The other night I was called on by a Tory councillor who said he wanted to re-introduce himself. I met him three years ago when he took copious notes of my complaint about the volume of heavy traffic invading the streets.

Three years is a long time to wait for an answer, but I was willing to listen. He had nothing to say, which is quite remarkable for a politician. Obviously his notes had ended up in the same place as the contents of my bins.

No matter. In three years' time he will still have the brass neck to introduce himself again, make more notes and soothing noises before seeking out the nearest waste paper basket. He wants my X but not my problems.

He is not alone. Wherever I have lived and worked I have met his counterparts. They have all had the same thing in common - the arrogant vanity to think they know better than those who elected them.

In one of those London boroughs famous for political tolerance, a teacher has just been publicly vilified for failing to attend a special Nelson Mandela assembly. Perhaps they will also give her a Goodyear Necklace.

That's the trouble with councillors. They won't allow you to choose your own heroes. I wouldn't give you two bob for the lot of them.

15 August, 1984

No swearing and not even a cross word

HAD ANYONE told me two years ago that I would now be squeezing my unsightly bulk into Bumble Bee Cottage to carry out a full physical check-up on Boober, I would have laughed.

I'd laugh now, but the energy just doesn't seem to be available. Becoming a father of two at my age - which is 40-mind-your-own-business - is rather like an amputee tackling Everest.

Gone are the slothful weekends devoted to the leisurely digestion of several newspapers and indulgent pub lunches. Weighty consideration of The Times crossword is now interrupted by demands that I draw a pussy cat or read the story of Little Pig's Birthday.

Or that I crawl into the colourful little tent to administer a placebo to the hypochondriacal Boober. For the uninitiated, Boober is an outrageously ugly orange and green felt toy with a gaping mouth.

Since he enjoys mega-star status on the TV series Fraggle Rock, his health is of prime importance. Since I do not enjoy playing doctors and nurses as much as I did 30 years ago, there have been days when he risked multiple fractures.

This leads to guilt feelings. Not because of one's sinister potential as a Fraggle batterer, rather because I'm supposed to enjoy sporting with the little gargoyle.

Everyone tells me that having children at my age will keep me young. In reality, this means having to shrug of the selfish, set ways of encroaching middle-age and to arrest a steadily contracting boredom threshold.

It means risking a coronary while huffily-puffily kicking a ball in the park and a hernia carrying the baby's bath. It means losing sleep, when you most need it, keeping your language in check when a howling match ruins you favourite TV show and being tolerant when a soggy rusk is wiped across your spectacles.

Having a notoriously weak stomach, I have to leave the room at nappy-changing time. I cringe when a gob of regurgitated milk leaves a slimy trail down my shirt. I yearn for those golden moments of peace when both have been convinced that they are in deep trouble with Wee Willie Winkie if they don't shut their little eyes and get off to sleep.

The daily whine, rattle and thump of the washing machine drives me bananas. My nerves are stretched taut by the 1,001 near-accidents which threaten the kids' crowns and bodies.

All this is meant to keep me young?

Yes, and it does. It all started in the delivery room when I endured the hell of the first birth. Admittedly, my wife also suffered some discomfort, but what a rewarding experience.

In the first 13 months of sleepless nights I learned to contain the welling rage that could so easily have made me a baby batterer. I now have more patience than at any time of my life. Although enjoying a marvellous capacity for doing absolutely nothing, I am more active than for many years and can whizz the double-buggy around the park with great alacrity.

I can be persuaded to get off my bottom and walk to the shop for a mere ten pence worth of jelly babies, or to create magnificent constructions with building bricks. At a push, I might even change dolly's clothes.

Where before my head would be buried in a book and my hand wrapped around a large scotch, now I play peep-bo over the bannister and pour orange juice into beakers. There are fleeting moments when I feel ridiculous - an aspiring man of letters diagnosing Boober's ailments or explaining the subtleties of Play Away.

But such sacrifices have their rewards. I give and receive a great deal of joy. My rapid progress towards total inertia has been arrested. My capacity for caring has increased five-fold and I like myself much better as a person.

I'll probably never manage to write the great novel, but hell, I feel I've already made my mark on life. My kids are the two most clever things I've ever done.

19 November, 1986

Knock, knock a man of letters

ALL THE gates in our street need oiling. They creak like mad. When you're lying abed at dawn and hear several creaks in quick succession then you know that Frank the harbinger of dire news, is on his way.

Lean as a greyhound and almost as fleet, Frank is our postman. We are on first name terms because he writes me such erudite notes in beautiful script. Just cast your eyes over this one.

"Dear John: A thousand pardons for taking liberties with your mail, but a packet of farinaceous comestibles for junior arrived this morning and, rather than drag you from the arms of Morpheus at this ungodly hour, and thereby excite Mrs Williams into visiting a certain familiarity upon my person in the shape of a straight left to the jaw, I've decided to take the coward's way out.

"You will find the aforesaid parcel fighting for its life amongst the aphids in your herbaceous border by the side of the front door at the end of the Primrose Path. O.K.? Postie."

He could simply have written that he had concealed a packet of baby gruel behind the shrub tubs, but our Frank has style. He also has a new dictionary with which, as an "antodidactic opsimath," he is slaking his thirst for our lyrical language.

Delighted as I am to have a postman with a far superior vocabulary, the fact remains that Frank - rather unfairly - is always associated with acute pains in the rear. He is the 1986 version of the 1940s bad-news telegram.

I see him as a dealer in begging letters and as a sinister agent for Readers' Digest, an organisation more difficult to shed than certain pernicious anti-social diseases. Surely a Nobel Prize awaits the man or woman who discovers an antidote to the mailing-list malaise.

When I met Frank by chance one day last week, I gleefully pointed out that he had slipped up rather badly by delivering some good tidings. Just for a change, the Inland Revenue had decided to give rather than take. How that must have hurt.

With a wicked grin which properly deserved a kick up the postbag, he said, "I'll soon put that right." So he did, silently sliding through the letterbox a polite request for £315 for mechanical repairs. Frank had shivved me in grand style.

My first instinct was to do a John Cleese by thrashing hell out of the car and screaming abuse at it. No profit in that. Like all motors it bears grudges and would surely have wreaked revenge within 48 hours. It's awfully spiteful.

I hate cars anyway. I've always hosted the conviction that whenever I have set foot on a garage forecourt some great Monty Pythonesque finger emerged from the heavens and hovered over my "room to let" head.

This enabled the salesman to easily recognise me as Mug of the Year and so rid his employers of the most craftily-disguised heap of garbage in stock. I've driven more rubbish than Ben Hur when it was the horses' day off.

Recently I was grievously saddened to read that a car dealer had been jailed. I was hoping for a much stiffer sentence than he was given since he had sold me the flash sports job which ran for six non-consecutive weeks in the space of three years.

There was the German executive model on which I had to take out an extension on the mortgage. It went back to the garage so often that I successfully demanded an invitation to the staff's Christmas party.

Then there was the ultimate crumpet-puller - the navy blue Alfa Romeo Spyder complete with wooden steering wheel. The crumpet successfully ignored me and the car gave off blue-black emissions of smoke sufficient to close motorways.

I did buy British on several occasions. One upmarket model - decidedly middle-aged in concept - had the unhappy knack of releasing several days of accumulated rainwater whenever I opened the glove compartment. It was sold to me by a relative.

So was the other expensive saloon which, without explanation, could slow itself down from 60 mph to 0 in the space of a few yards. None of the car doctors I consulted could make an adequate diagnosis. The relative moved house.

My current model is still gloating over its unscheduled seven-hour stop on the hard shoulder of the Ml as we made our way to Dover. We got it to work, but it paid us back by reversing into a French tree. Doubtless an act for sympathy with indigenous lamb producers.

Frank, who rides a bike has fewer problems. He merely delivers them and leaves you to rot. After scouring three dictionaries, I really must rise at dawn one day and ask him what on earth "antodidactic" means. You can learn a lot from your Postie.

20 September, 1989

Salivating for blood with the jackals ...

DID YOU ever see a soul quit its shell? The seepage of life from a body leaves you bowed by indescribable sadness. You are left with the pallid husk of a being and the memory of a death rattle which assails your senses for years to come.

If you have lived through that experience, as did I, it is indelibly imprinted on your mind's micro-chip and will not go away. To watch someone lose that which is most precious to them is Nature's most sobering and inexorable rite.

Obviously, it hurts more if the person was someone dear to you. But to see even a total stranger expiring takes the stiffening out of your shins. It reminds you of the value of life and how fragile is your own mortality.

To watch it ooze away and flee to its supposed celestial home is one thing. To hasten or bring about its demise is quite another. Is that not murder, the most heinous of crimes?

I raise the question because Mrs Thatcher has reportedly called for the return of the death penalty for police killers following last week's shooting of an officer at an M62 service station.

To me it sounded like a bit of cynical vote-catching, easily said and done in the comfortable knowledge that the Commons is unlikely to endorse such a measure. The Honourable Members have long been consistent in their opposition to hanging.

They have flown in the face of savagely primordial public opinion which yelps and bays for blood and revenge. It is the instinct of the jackal, a base desire to take life for the sake of a corkscrewed mentality.

Calculated murder by the state is no better than the act for which a person hangs. It is premeditated, cold-blooded, institutionalised killing which has no place in any nation pleased to call itself civilised.

I was at Chester Assizes to see experienced policemen weep openly when Lesley Ann Downey's anguished pleas for her mother were played from a tape recorder. At that moment, anyone in the court would have gladly despatched Brady and Hindley.

It was only days later when my revulsion and pain had subsided that I realised such an act would drag me down to the level of that wicked couple. Like them, I would be a killer.

Where would lie the distinction? Surely not in legal sanction, a mere device to justify the primitive proclivity within me and others. I wished Brady and Hindley dead, but preferably by their own hands, or by the course of nature.

The burden of taking life must lie heavily on those charged with the gruesome duty, unless they are as surrealistically detached as was Albert Pierrepoint, the public hangman.

To him it was simply a job. He spied through little holes to size up the prisoner, adjusted the weights on his rope and pulled the lever. He took inordinate pride in doing a "clean job."

Timothy Evans, of 10 Rillington Place, must have been pleased about that. I'll bet he was even more knocked out by his posthumous pardon. Mind you, it did little to enhance the quality of his life.

There is still a big question mark, posed by the redoubtable Ludovic Kennedy, over the guilt of James Hanratty. But we cannot bring him back, no more than we can recall any other wrongly found guilty.

This is one of the inherent dangers of a terribly final act. Circumstantial evidence, or that which is sometimes tampered with, can have dreadful consequences as things are without putting someone to death.

I cannot agree with those who argue that the ultimate sentence is a deterrent. If that were so, there should have been many fewer murders when the ghastly system was in operation.

People kill mostly through panic, desperation, blind hatred or because they are unbalanced. The state kills in cold blood which, for me, has sinister overtones. Revenge is a distortion.

Neither do I subscribe to the theory of selective execution. If murder was to be punishable by death, it should apply to all and not just those who slay police officers. Otherwise we should be living with an insufferable and undemocratic anomaly.

Some deaths are more grisly than others and it would be wrong, under those hypothetical circumstances for the perpetrator of a truly horrible crime to escape with his life simply because his victim was not a policeman.

However, thank goodness the question does not arise. In its often questionable wisdom, Parliament decided that we should leave behind the dark days of the noose and get in step with civilisation.

Douglas Hurd, the Home Secretary, has pointed out that no police killer has left prison alive since capital punishment ended 25 years ago. That, I suggest, is a living death and should be enough to satisfy society's demands.

15 October, 1985

A walk on the vile side

NO DOUBT hoping for a quick sale to the Arts Council's idiot-in-residence, someone has at last removed the Kwiksave trolley from the lake in our park. It had lain there half submerged for months until its potential as a "Raising of the Belgrano" was spotted.

The red-brick connurbation surrounding this verdant oasis is not a noted centre of culture, but there is many a canny soul with an eye to a fast buck. If a sardine can in a zinc bath is worth £600, what price an algae-festooned transporter of comestibles?

While it may yet take its place alongside the infamous pile of bricks, the heap of coal and other visual jokes purchased for a strangely ungrateful nation, its disappearance has done little to enhance the lake. Wildfowl and water lily alike are mugged by a floating collage of all the detritus known to man.

Into this corner-shop jetsam small boys cast their nylon lines in quest of anything that may still be alive beneath the bestrewn and murky surface. Bored by his lack of success, an angler not much bigger than a pocket calculator is trying to smash a milk bottle. I offer advice about the safety of others and he, in his piping Pollyanna voice, suggests I go away and perform a physical impossibility.

I then try offering advice about his own safety by threatening to clack him one. He senses a bluff and emboldened by the vocal support of his little friends repeats the suggestion. His backers are making embarrassing allegations about my private life so I decide to leave, sad that a seven-year-old is already a mature yob.

On the other side of the lake a goose is waddling along the path as if it has just had a good night out on Australian sherry. In fact it is in great pain. A length of fishing line is wrapped around one leg and cutting into the flesh. I report its distress to a patrolling policeman.

"Oh, I think we'd better leave it alone," he says brimming over with indifference. I point out that inaction will lead to amputation and that artificial limbs for geese are hard to come by. He promises to inform the RSPCA and ambles away to chat up two young girls. If it's left to him, the bird's goose is cooked.

There is other wildlife in the park and they're all tearing around on BMX bikes like the sons of the O'Hooligans. A man who might be the park-keeper shouts angrily and they circle him like a pack of jackals. He sets off in pursuit, but they easily evade him. All he catches is an earful of abuse.

The pale autumn sun has brought out a whole posse of the Lesser Checked Grass Walker. This species is entirely female and middle-aged, wears discreetly patterned tweed skirts, sensible shoes and is always trailed by something which looks like a badly knitted scouring pad.

This, of course, is her pet dog. It is a characteristic of Walkers that they believe their animals to be human, in constant need of smothering affection and conversation dotted with words like "darling" and "sweetheart." If the dog plays its cards right, it usually gets carried most of the way home.

Another trait is the consideration Walkers show to each other's shoes. They never allow Sweetie to do a whoopsie on the paths, always in the grass so the rancid coils are concealed from children who might want to gambol.

One day, if I can summon up the courage, I intend to stand in the middle of the park and bellow "King" and "Sheba." If my theory is correct, I would then be surrounded by at least 15 Alsatians, Dobermans and - the latest macho status symbol - Rotweillers.

These are usually accompanied by young men clad in black leather and denim who cannot read. At least, I suppose that to be the case because it is always under the notice which decrees that all dogs must be on a leash that these great, lolloping mutts are set free.

A particularly proud owner will try to draw attention to himself by demonstrating that he has watched at least two Barbara Woodhouse programmes and has complete control over his charge. Thus when he cries, "Sheba, come," you can expect the dog to run the other way and pin a pensioner to a tree or mow a kid down.

Some owners are more successful in their training methods. Over at the children's play area a young mother was warning other parents to keep their tots off the slide. Right on the spot where they plonk their little bums to begin the descent was a dollop of dog dirt.

One exuberant child did not hear the warning and launched himself down the chute. I walked over to his mother and discreetly told her the likely state of the boy's trousers. She looked at me as if I were the stuff he had sat in and said absolutely nothing. Funny woman.

A hop, skip and a jump away there was a football match in progress so I paused to take in a vignette of honest, amateur sporting endeavour. There was the usual speculation about the referee's lineage from the crowd of about 50, but that was only when the game was being played in a reasonably civilised way.

When it got rough, faces contorted with rage, voices rose a couple of octaves and obscenities flew as thick as the arrows during that ancient dust-up at Hastings. A couple embedded themselves in my conscience because there were children nearby. I didn't want to be seen in bad company.

Miffed that their previous efforts had been erased, the graffiti artists had struck again at the cricket pavilion. Its white facade now bears the garish green legend 'Killer.' It could, I suppose, have been put there by the pace bowler as a psychological tactic.

As I picked my way through the carpet of chip wrappers at the exit, I spotted my little fisherman friend across the road. He seemed to have heeded my advice because he still had the milk bottle. Then he smashed it in the path of oncoming traffic and ran off laughing.

I enjoy my walks in the park. You meet some really nice people in a sylvan setting.

22 February, 1989

Word-perfect obituary of a mistress

DISPLAYING MORE than élan than a Vogue covergirl, Clever Clogs (aka 'Er Indoors) last week committed murder. It was not a wilful act, but, nevertheless, robbed me of an old friend and a demanding mistress. She killed my old typewriter.

"I think something's wrong with it," she said after dropping its considerable weight on the study floor.

This utterance was a variation of her usual phrase - "It just came away in my hand" - employed to explain away her daily acts of vandalism. She treats crockery as if it were made of cast-iron.

The writing machine was taken to a sympathetic shop where rigor mortis was confirmed. I almost wept, for I could never walk by her without wanting to insert a virginal sheet of paper and strum her still nimble limbs. Ours was a true love affair.

I took the body back to the car and gave Clever Clogs the sort of affectionate glance Khomeini reserves for Rushdie. "It's only fit for scrap now," I snarled. "Never mind," she smiled, while maintaining a safe distance between us.

Next day she came home with a huge box which, she assured me, would solve all our letter-writing and working problems. Not only that, but it would equip the children with technological knowledge to prepare them for their Wellsian futures. It was a word processor.

If you heed the hype, this box of tricks is meant to make life a damned sight easier. Presumably that is why it comes with an operating manual nearly two inches thick written in a language which only approximates the tongue common to most of us.

In trying to master the very basics, I spat out words that would have curdled milk. My only early success was in conjuring up on the screen "ERROR." I took this to be a reference to Clever Clogs's initiative in buying the thing. She, of course, managed to produce work in minutes, a quality which makes her such a great and superior irritant. But then came the complex matter of programming the floppy disc, an accessory which proved to be the progeny of unwed parents.

"Remove disc and continue by hitting any key," read the oft-repeated message. The screen was chocabloc with obscure or impenetrably dopey instructions, which brought no results. I've seldom heard such colourful language, except when that depraved Tawny Owl used to telephone me late at night.

Clogs sacrificed a whole afternoon in trying to enter the files she had created. Eventually, calling upon her Corps Diplomatique experience, she exclaimed, "Well you try reading the bloody book." It didn't help when I laughed. Relations were temporarily frozen.

So was the floppy thing which, days on, we have yet to master. However, I successfully managed to produce this modest ouvrage before transferring it to the sophisticated Cyclops which occupies my office desk for direct inputting into a central computer.

It's so sophisticated that it has its own black holes down which one's copy can disappear forever, if precautions are not taken. It's at times like those you miss the primitive typewriter, which only ever needed a new ribbon unless your wife decided to commit homicide.

I truly do not comprehend a machine which, instructions faithfully followed, prints the first line of my address on the right then resolutely buzzes off to the extreme left of the stationery for the remainder. Perhaps it was assembled by socialists.

Cheap jokes apart, now I can use the thing for basic tasks I find it almost exciting. It is now so easy to edit one's work and has eliminated the need for swearing while tearing a ruined sheet of A4 from the typewriter's roller. The old machine is a dinosaur.

My children will benefit, too. Even as someone who rejoices in the mini-revival of the beautiful fountain-pen, I shall school them in emergent technology so they are at least familiar with its bones. No doubt they will soon be instructing me.

It is the young, rather than the meek, who shall inherit the material Earth. Pliable minds can cope with innovations easier than those of us steeped in long-practised skills which are dying with the birth of each new menu of chip ingenuity.

The changes are both invigorating and sad. For every chip that can do a trick, lots of people end up alongside my typewriter - on the scrapheap. I like my new magic box, but what about the guy who put together my tired Remington? Is he redundant or dead?

Clogs wants to make an insurance claim on the fruits of his labour. She asked about its replacement value and was given lots of ers and ums. "They just don't make them any more," she was told. That's destructive progress for you.

Now the chip is cock-of-the-walk - until some genius makes a quantum leap forward.

But I still love nine-carat gold nibs and the way they caress and decorate a leaf of paper. No friend of mine will ever receive a letter written on this glaring green screen, and my pen will never issue a hiss and a sigh and wipe out my words in a frenzy of static.

4 June, 1987

Class of '87: Not so bright

YOU WOULD have to be daft, drunk or delirious not to see through the thinly disguised political propaganda which has just been shoved through your front door by the National Union of Teachers.

It is headed, "For all our children, vote for education." This, presumably, is a specific reference to those times when they are not engaged in staging half-day strikes. Teaching is a caring profession.

It is difficult to vote for education when, at lunch-time, tutors are donning their dull anoraks and abandoning their jobs and young charges. You cannot learn much when Sir and Miss have paid obeisance to their union commissars.

At a time when potential employers are complaining that applicants are barely conversant with their native tongue, it ill behoves the NUT to leap upon its pious hobby horse.

It is also difficult to vote for education when, for instance, in Wirral the Labour spokesman advocates aiming for a middle course rather than academic excellence. What a shrewd man. Who needs to be smart when mediocrity satisfies the local council?

It becomes more difficult when you know that at least two members of the ruling party send their children to private schools but want the finer grammar schools abolished. The stench of hypocrisy blocks your nostrils.

There is the naive assumption that all children are equal, no matter how dim or retarded. The brains of the class must mark time while the dimbos try in vain to catch up. What bloody nonsense.

What is fundamentally wrong with a system devoted to encouraging and developing young minds full of promise? Surely not that lesser minds will feel inferior or deprived. You must have a better reason than that for suppressing the gifted.

How else will they contribute to society unless they are taken to one side to have their grey cells nurtured, massaged and expanded? Like muscles and the heart, the brain needs to be exercised.

The notional aim of equality, despite yawning gulfs in intellect, is born out of political ideology rather than reality. Which genius can flourish in a garden full of weeds? Put him in the hothouse.

Not that too many of our teachers are capable of nursing exotic blooms. Most belong in the profession because it is a job rather than a vocation. The letters I get from my eldest daughter's school bristle with grammatical errors.

Still if you pay peanuts you must expect to employ a few monkeys. When you entrust a young mind to the influences of another that person should be brilliant and impartial and should be amply rewarded for being so.

I well remember helping a young friend who was required to write an essay on the disease of bilharzia. Using my connections, I tapped the admirable expertise of Liverpool's School of Tropical Medicine.

The teacher awarded her a B grade. Better informed on the subject than he, she complained and was swiftly awarded an A. Would you want your child's mind in his hands?

And have you ever watched news clips of NUT industrial action meetings? How can children have respect for those who look as if they have been dressed in Oxfam designer gear? Their very apparel shouts out their political philosophy.

They are scruffs espousing the causes of the Left. The document shoved through my letter-box was meant to be clever and subtle. It betrayed the intellectual shortcomings of the NUT. My children are at their mercy.

When I was a Jack-the-lad youth I aided three young women to enter the profession by writing their final theses. They didn't have the *nous*. I did, and now they are teachers. What a fool I was.

I did it because they had nice legs and chests. You know how it is when you are young and impressionable. Today, I would commit suicide if I thought any one of them was attempting to mould the thinking of my offspring. They were dimmer than a guttering candle.

God save us from politicians - local or national - who believe that all people are equal. Are you equal to a Chelsea football supporter, a mugger or a rapist? Are you equal to a burglar, car thief, fraudster or someone whose IQ is less than half yours?

Of course not. Educationalists still need to sift, to separate wheat from chaff so that those with imagination will not be held back by those whose idea of a good time is to maim or scar a Millwall follower. To have them in the same class is madness.

The NUT's propaganda is blatantly political, despite the semantics. They have an axe to grind and chose a critical time at which to do it. They will only fool those who are stupid or are already of their persuasion.

. . . .

AT THE weekend I walked into a shop and saw a woman paying for her purchases. "Gosh," I said in a loud voice. "You're attractive. Any chance of sharing your bed tonight?"

She laughed and said, "No. Push off." I knew she was bluffing because I had been sleeping with her for eight years except for the nights when I've been consigned to the spare room. Wives have their difficult moments.

What I most enjoyed about the encounter was the look on the face of the counter assistant. I love to shock. Anyway, I bought my wife a bunch of tiger lilies which she planted in a milk bottle by the the kitchen sink. Who said romance was dead?

18 May, 1988

Voices in my ear that will not go away

MOST OF you will now be familiar with the contemporary version of Archimedes' law. Forget about the displacement of water. This rendition has it that the moment you submerge a body in a hot bath, the damned phone will start ringing.

More often than not, it seems to me, the caller will be Kitchens Direct, a company whose antecedents probably owe much to the ruthless tenacity of the Chinese Tongs. Their concept of mercy was a single bullet through the brain after prolonged bouts of water torture.

Kitchens Direct are less compassionate. They were not even shaken when I brusquely told them that they were more difficult to shed than herpes.

Naively, I thought I had delivered the killer blow when I said they were welcome to survey my scullery if they bore in mind that I had not even a wooden nickel to spare. Did you ever try killing a stone?

There I was supine on the sofa, contemplating the uncertain whereabouts of my navel, when the phone rang at 9 pm. A voice said, "Hello, I'm Karen and I work for Kitchens Direct. We're offering a free service by sending design experts to come and look at your kitchen."

Poor girl. She got an earful without even mentioning that her real motive was to part me from a load of loot - between three or four grand for the twee aggrandisement of the space in which my wife casts culinary spells.

I was frank. "Look," I sighed. "I recognise every sales pitch that's ever been conceived. I've spoken to your people so often you ought to include me on your office Christmas party guest list.

"I've just spent a large fortune on a new bathroom and it will be two years before I can afford the next bar of soap. By all means send your expert, but warn him that if he finds fivepence behind the cooker, I'll fight him to the death for it."

Could I have made it plainer? With commendable aplomb, Karen turned aside from the telephone and told someone, "He's interested but he's got no money." I felt both cheap and jubilant - mostly cheap.

Surely this would get them off my back? Karen came back with, "Would Wednesday evening be all right?" My flabber has never been so gasted. Do you see what I mean about herpes?

"You will both be in?" she inquired. "Yes," I said, "and we'll both have no money." Karen proved to be as yielding as a Sherman tank, but I reasoned that the designer would see the futility of trying to flog tarted-up pine and Formica to a mendicant.

I started writing this piece immediately, only to be interrupted at 9.30 pm. by Alison, Karen's supervisor. KD don't mind if you're making whoopee on the settee, entertaining, having a late dinner or doing a crossword in the loo. They always find time to give you a call.

Alison was sweet. She apologised for having subjected me to an inexperienced canvasser and reluctantly agreed that I was a hopeless prospect. What she would not concede was this was about the eighth call I had taken from KD.

"We'd have crossed you off," she said in patronising tones. "Sorry to have bothered you, but is it all right if we call back in two years time?" The herpes factor again.

KD must have their own celestial calendars. Those two years flashed by in only 72 hours according to my earthly clock. "Is our appointment still on?" asked Mr Design Expert. He was clearly chastened by a flat "no" which took a lengthy string of rude words to convey.

The point of this saga is that direct selling is an offensive invasion of one's privacy at the most inconvenient times. Subtle techniques of auto-suggestion are used to persuade people to buy goods they either do not want or cannot afford.

My wife foolishly admitted a vacuum cleaner salesman for a promised maximum of 20 minutes. It took that long to assemble the gear, a similar time for the demo and the same again to stow it away. Awaiting my dinner, I was overjoyed.

It was a truly wondrous machine having only two noticeable drawbacks. Firstly it could not be tuned into Radio Luxembourg and secondly, it cost £800. When the man started probing our incomes I staged my own demo by showing him to the front door.

Another doorstep caller wanted to know if I had any old clothes. "Yes, but I'm not getting undressed for you," I said. What about scrap metal, he asked, so I told him we still cooked on it and if he was interested in antiques my relatives were not for sale.

Replacement windows, chamois leathers and dusters, religion, ghastly pictures etched in copper and brass, vulgar stone cladding - all these and more can be bought at the front door. One man's castle is another's point of sale.

I'm saving up until my bell is rung by someone selling peace and privacy. I'll buy him out lock, stock and barrel.

3 December, 1986

Why I'm voting labour again

GIVING BIRTH is a horrendously painful business. Yet quite bravely, I am determined to have another baby. Since she will play a marginal role in this major miracle, I fully intend enlisting the aid and co-operation of Mrs Williams. The leggy, sassy minx.

Did you ever see a baby being born? It emerges covered in all sorts of gunge and starts bawling almost immediately but, God, it's a beautiful sight. The only thing you can do is shed a few tears of joy and congratulate yourself on being one of the world's best genetic engineers.

And it's such a relief after all those agonising hours of labour, the anguish, the travail. At times it was sheer hell but, being preoccupied, my wife didn't seem to notice what I was going through.

I have this lingering memory of the moans, the groans and the howling; of my tiny hand being crushed in hers with every wracking spasm. Will I ever be able to play the violin again, I wondered, expecting the digits to end up like a small pile of Ready-Brek.

She was wired up to some visual display unit which monitored the unborn baby's heartbeat. It flickered like mad and the sound was what you would expect from a herd of Shetland ponies fleeing an uncompromising representative of a knacker's yard.

While Mrs W was undergoing a modicum of discomfort, my nerve-ends had unravelled and were snaking all over the floor. She seemed curiously impervious. How could she do this to me? For goodness sake, all she had to do was pop the little mite out.

After five hours I could take no more. "I'm just going out for some fresh air," I said and headed for the smoke-filled bar of the nearest pub for a large measure of Dutch courage. Fresh air's fine in its place, but those heart-rending yelps were still assailing my ears and I needed a drop of anaesthetic.

We had woken at such an early hour that my first instinct had beento offer my wife the car keys and turn over. Now fatigue had set in and the Scotch hit me like an Exocet, revealing an awful truth. I was chicken.

Not even someone else's pain could I bear.

Another whisky and several cigarettes later I really could no longer prolong the agony. In a rare burst of religious fervour I said out loud, "Please God, let it be all over when I get back." The women at the next table clearly thought they were in the company of an inebriated Welsh Asbestos Methodist.

It wasn't all over, and a maddeningly cheerful nurse said it was all right for me to go back into the labour room. There she was, still in that undignified position, obviously distressed and emitting several more decibels than before. Now I needed a real anaesthetic.

They gave me one of those Dr Kildare gowns and a face mask and assured me there was nothing to worry about. "It's always like this," said the cheerful one and I decide there and then that when this baby deigned to turn up, it was going to be an only child. I wasn't up to another birth.

Neither was I prepared for what happened next. All that straining was getting us nowhere because the infant's head was out of alignment (and she's been an awkward monkey ever since.) It was going to be a scalpel and forceps job. My scalp prickled because there wasn't enough hair to stand on end. Not blood on top of everything else!

"You'll be wanting me to go outside then?" I hopefully asked the doctor. With a callous indifference to the elements of poultry within me he said it was perfectly all right to remain.

I've not had so much fun since breaking an arm. I averted my face and gave my wife a hug that was meant to comfort her, but which actually was more to prevent me falling over. In fairness to the doctor, I didn't feel a thing and the baby entered the world in a trice. I'd done it at last.

After ten hours of painful thrashing around, Mrs W did not look her best. But when they gave her the baby to hold she looked gorgeous and I finally understood what it is about birth that makes grown men - or in my case, half-grown - go all dewy-eyed. After all the work's been done for them, of course.

The unpleasant memories of that day soon faded, until we discovered that a second child was on the way. Whoopee! Another fun-filled day in that room to look forward to. My wife said that she would again like a strong, consoling figure at her side, but would make do with me.

As luck would have it, I was tied up with work on that eventful day. Thehospital rang to say that if I wanted to see the baby born, I would have to hurry. You've never seen anyone hurry in such leisurely fashion. It was three minutes old when I arrived.

The first minute of the first birth had been beautiful, but it was the preceding hours which dwelt on my mind as I drove to the hospital for the second. I had chickened out and have regretted it ever since.

So now I have two girls, fashioned in the image of angels and with the battling instincts of Al Capone. They have illuminated my middle years, given life a vestige of meaning and often drive me crackers.

There are days when you would think they were rehearsing for the lead roles in a remake of Whatever Happened to Baby Jane? and others when a smile from either can make your heart lurch. There are never dull days.

More than four years have passed since the eldest was born, and Number Two is pushing three. I think I'm getting broody. Or maybe it's because age is creeping up on me and I'd like to leave behind another living reminder that I once trod this land.

Whichever, negotiations are at the tentative stage and I think I might be wining. If so, next time I'll really try hard to get to hospital on time.

16 November, 1988

Prejudice that refuses to obey law or logic

YOU NEED to be a special sort of person to be offended by the depiction of a black-faced doll on a jar of marmalade. Firstly, it helps if you are white, stuffily monocular and up to the eyebrows in liberal pretension.

Being a bit daft is a definite aid and there is a real bonus to be had from being partially deaf. This enables you to ignore the wall of indifferent silence emanating from a cheerful black community which has little time for such trivia.

Lastly, and ideally, you should not be gainfully employed. This allows oodles of spare time in which to convince yourself that what people spread on their toast is a sticky time-bomb which could lead to violent demonstrations outside Robertsons' jam factories.

While waiting in vain for the inflammatory thick orange cut to cause social unrest, you could ponder alternative campaigns. Why not inveigh against the caricatures to be found on goods in Chinatown's supermarket? You can always overlook the fact that the logos were designed by the Chinese, who have never once figured in the race industry's fashionable causes.

Indeed, you could even ponder why, in a multi-racial society, ethnic groups other than blacks seldom if ever if ever get a mention. Ask any Jew who's been turned down for membership by those snooty golf clubs which operate discreet, but odious anti-Semitic policies.

There is always a conspicuous absence of bleeding hearts on the first tee and cudgels are laid to rest. No arms are raised in horror and no ringing speeches echo through the council chamber. Why should this be?

I suspect it is because, just as the golliwog is meant to stereotype the black, the Jew remains a victim of the image projected by Shylock and the positively evil propaganda put about by Hitler and Goebbels. But he has few champions among those who can clearly see black but are blind to the rainbow of humanity.

Over dinner one night I provoked what became a heated debate with an avowedly anti-racist couple. It's one way of finding out what people really think. We trotted out our respective arguments, mine being that racism has, and always will be, part of man's make-up.

Naturally, they disagreed and later left me bereft of oxygen by announcing that they were cancelling their planned holiday in the Holy Land because they detested Jews. An extreme example of how selective the anti-race business can be.

Just look at India's wholly laughable stance against playing cricket with Englishmen who have visited South Africa. Strictly speaking, apartheid means separate development. In practice it means blatant discrimination which in India is ruthlessly applied through the infamous caste system.

There is no development, separate or otherwise, for those who must devote their lives to menial and demeaning tasks and will forever be saddled with that less than charming soubriquet, The Untouchables. That's hardly cricket.

Sri Lankans and Tamils are not the best of mates and you'll see very few Arabs walking hand in hand with Israelis. The Egyptians went wild when Omar Shariff planted a big swoopie on Barbra Streisand's lips during a film, and Beirut is hardly free of bigotry.

The Chinese and Japanese have a low opinion of "round-eyes", Germans seem to be born with a racial superiority complex and I know a Roman Catholic priest who despises the Italians and all "spineless" peoples who work with the sun on their backs.

There are writers on The Times, the supposed paradigm of all that is good and honest in journalism, who have a pronounced aversion to the Welsh. "Fancy having to ask a friend if she were both lesbian *and* Welsh," is one snide comment which springs to mind.

In turn, some Welsh demonstrate their tolerance with childishly irresponsible acts of arson. The English are not their favourite neighbours although they prop up the service industries which depend on the tourist trade. Bilingualism becomes essential when accepting visitors' money.

I think my laboured point has been made. You can have all the legislation in the world and a race commissar planted on every street and nothing will change. Nearly 400 years after Shakespeare wrote the spitefully anti-Semitic The Merchant of Venice, sporting gentlemen golfers are perpetuating the prejudice.

The Commission for Racial Equality is largely a waste of time and money and its handful of victories in cases it could not lose were pyrrhic. A bigoted employer will always find an excuse to turn down applicants of whatever colour. There is always the possibility, too, that they are unsuitable for the post but will ascribe their failure to prejudice.

I well remember being described by a mountainous black as being "a typical honky white-trash racist." I took the flattery in my stride. It did not seem unreasonable in the middle of a working day to refuse to drive 30 miles out of my way to give him a lift.

The pity of it is that the "industry", urged on by those who wage war on marmalade jar labels, now industriously seeks out racism in perfectly innocent and impartial act. That is why Enid Blyton's books have been banned from some libraries and excluded from the Government's proposed shake-up of teaching methods.

The poor old golliwog is back in the mire. Daft, isn't it?

29 October, 1986

When the kissing has to stop ...

IN THE unlikely event that I ever have £2,000 to spare (or even five bob, come to that), I would certainly not use it to finance a foreign holiday for a prostitute I had never even met. I'm funny that way.

Call me mean if you will, but I do not possess the philanthropic spirit and disposable income of Jeffrey Archer. However, what he does with his loot is between him and God, who is currently living in Downing Street with a test pilot for Gordon's Gin.

My spare cash is reserved for the string of men who regularly troop to the front door to fulfil my wife's fantasies. She has this recurring dream that everything in the house should be in proper working order and that anything paintable should regularly be dipped in two coats of gloss.

Nominally, I am the man of the house but it's a role which clashes with my heaven-sent gift for total lethargy. Mentally, I indulge in much navel contemplation, worry about 1 Across, weigh up the merits of Irish whiskey as opposed to Scotch and wonder what Esther Rantzen does with her teeth at night.

While there are heaps of other equally important matters to be mulled over, there hardly seems time to be messing around with screw-drivers, spanners, brushes, putty, plastic wood, electric drills and all the other paraphernalia which is part of the house-husband's image.

I'm a thinker. I keep thinking I should get off my bum and do something, but the potent combination of indolence and fear renders me as immobile as Rodin's statue. The fear stems from the prospect of making a complete idiot of myself yet again.

Not that my wife is unsympathetic. We were doing a spot of necking in the kitchen when her gaze wandered to some unfinished task hanging off the wall. Our lips parted long enough for her to look me tenderly in the eye and murmur, "You're bloody hopeless."

In view of the almost infinite limits of my incompetence at things practical, her remark almost ranked as a compliment. She recognises that I am a graduate of the Frank Spencer (Some Mothers Do Have 'Em)

School of D-I-Y.

Only last week I suggested I might fill the space beneath the bay window by constructing something in wood that we could fill with a colourful mass of pot plants. I wouldn't have got round to it, of course, but she said nothing for several minutes.

This was because she was rendered speechless by an uncontrollable fit of laughter which left her clutching her stomach in a paroxysm of agony. I knew instinctively that she was remembering The Great Pelmet Incident.

Encouraged by one of those clever Dicks who can do anything and everything, I successfully joined together four bits of wood and rawl plugged them to the wall. Suffused with pride I invited her upstairs for the curtain opening ceremony.

She was visibly impressed. Making a grandiloquent gesture with my left hand, I gently tugged at the cord with my right. What a moment. The right side of the pelmet left its moorings, struck me on the head and left me with a close-up view of the carpet. I do not recall which hurt the more - the tumbling timber or the mirth rattling in my ears.

Then there was the bedside telephone table-cum-bookcase which was found on the floor after fulfilling its function for less than 24 hours. Mrs Williams just will not accept that inferior plasterwork is to blame.

Nor will she understand that walls are never straight. She points to my wallpapering and rather cruelly emphasises that not only can you see the joins but they are on a greater slant than Charlie Chan's eyes. I mean, did I build the wall?

I'm a romantic not an artisan. I gaze at that lissom body, those endless legs (shame about the patellas) and consider drowning of ecstasy in those grey eyes of hers. Inside I'm screaming, "Stop letting bits of vegetables go down the sink because I don't know how to unclog S-bends."

I dread those moments when something goes wrong and it is assumed, purely on the basis of gender, that I shall be the one to sort it out. Why does the lavatory seat keep falling off? I am frequently asked. Who knows what goes on behind closed doors?

Is it my fault that after thrice being fixed, the catch on the front gate is crazily out of alignment with the latch? Am I to blame because the binmen can no longer open the back gate since it benefited from my handiwork? Of course.

That is why, too, it is impossible to brew a cup of coffee without repeatedly bashing the plug to keep the percolator operating. It's been wired so often I could stroll into membership of the EEPTU.

Before Saturday night, when we are having a dinner party, I really should do something about the old dining table, but I reckon that after a few minutes the guests will accustom themselves to the very real feeling that they are aboard an ocean-going liner.

Best to leave it to the growing number of tradesmen who now ring our bell, although they tend to demonstrate that some plasterwork is quite sound, some walls are virtually straight and that wiring up some appliance need not be done to the accompaniment of rude words.

The trouble is, it all costs money. Perhaps I should tart myself up and give that kind Mr Archer a tinkle.

31 December, 1986

Putting your first foot in it

IN MY YOUNG days (when I had sufficient hair to justify being described as dark) some neighbours weighed me down with a quite hefty lump of coal and invited me to do a spot of first-footing.

With my track record, they'd have been better off asking the ancient mariner to let his pet albatross make a quick circuit of the front room. Still, who can resist being cast as the harbinger of good luck?

So, toting my black nugget, I crossed their threshold, made a quick appraisal of the furniture and decor (quite tatty), and exited stage left through the back door. I had ushered in their New Year.

Two positive things emerged from this superstitious ritual. Firstly, I got dirty hands. Secondly, the couple went through a scandalous and acrimonious divorce only months later. As harbingers go, I was clearly a bit duff.

It was possible my first real indication that merely flicking over the page of a calendar was not enough to prevent Life aiming a size 12 boot at one's squelchy bits. The Great Architect of Trouble and Strife doesn't give a damn what year it is.

Neither do I. December 31 always brings a fit of inexplicable melancholia. I invariably feel the need to reach for the nearest Jehovah's Witness and inquire if Armageddon has arrived yet again. It would be a good time to end the world.

Not that the Scots would be pleased. Tonight they'll all be swigging gallons of whisky from hollowed-out haggises and involuntarily lying down to avoid being spotted by rampant herds of pastel-coloured elephants.

The few who remain standing - the likes of Andy Stewart and Moira Anderson - will undoubtedly pop up on the box to render our sporrans rigid with boredom. Televised Hogmanay is hogwash. It's all dirks, kilts and Donald Where's Yer Trewsers?

We get invited to parties, but rarely go. Have you ever tried to get a baby sitter on New Year's Eve? Not that I mind. I despise all that bonhomie, generated by oodles of the hard stuff, which is as real as a five-bob note.

The chimes of midnight signal an orgy of face sucking, surreptitious groping and the release of a year's pent-up lust. Lots of secret passions emerge as the cartoonist's grizzled Father Time makes way for the baby with his giant egg-timer.

In reality, they're kissing goodbye to another year of their lives and girding their loins for whatever the fates will throw at them in the coming 12 months. Life is but a series of crises punctuated by fleeting moments of tranquillity.

So tonight, while all around me are merrily donating their livers to Bacchus, I, hopefully, will be sonorously snoring. It's as well to get in some sleep before being woken in the small hours by home-going revellers up to their gills in booze.

Or maybe I'll be up and about reassuring the children that the rock music emanating from the house ten doors away will stop some time short of breakfast. You can attend some parties without getting out of bed.

My New Year's resolution is not to make one. This is to spare me the embarrassment, as in previous years, of having broken it by 10 am on January 1. When it comes to will-power I have all the strength of a cup of tea brewed by British Rail.

I recall reading last year a very convincing piece by a colleague about the dangers of smoking. It was his resolution to kick the weed into touch. So firm was his resolve that, 12 months on he is down to 40 a day. A man of iron.

Any new year is a meaningless abstract, the turn of the calendar bolstered by our largely futile hopes that bleak mid-winter's bills will not be totally crippling and that our inevitable trials and tribulations will not be insurmountable.

Like primitives, we stage the rite of the drunken knees-up to ward off evil spirits - oblivious to the fact that we are actually drinking some of them. But, as every year reminds one, you can't keep a good evil spirit down.

This time around, New Year's Eve might have been different had not my Christmas house guest, of whom I wrote last week, returned to Hastings. Edna Sweet was delightfully different, a vaguely bohemian septuagenarian.

I shall never forget seeing her off at Lime Street Station. She strode on to Platform 7, put down her luggage and gave the engine an affectionate pat. "Have a safe journey," she told it. There were those who looked askance but, by this time, I was fully used to her endearingly batty ways.

She has since written a letter of thanks which ended with the words, "I miss you and your love, but I'm glad I didn't miss you and your love." It was a line borrowed from my wife's book of poems.

It meant more to me than all the hollow exhortations which will be flying about just after midnight. Edna likes the occasion. I don't, but I'm sure if she were here I'd have been tempted to raise a brimming glass and say, "Happy New Year."

13 June, 1990

Mercenary territory for the lovelorn

FROM A COMMANDING position flat on my back clad in pyjamas and caparisoned in ennui, I was able to study the ceiling in great detail. As a visual experience it ranked alongside watching Cyril Smith getting undressed.

Then my view was blocked by a quite lovely face. Its owner, wearing a smile borrowed from Circe, half whispered these sweet words: "Mr Williams, I have to tell you that you are treading on a knife edge."

How like a doctor to first soften you up with the good news before zapping you with the messy stuff. Only the force of gravity prevented me from doing a Lazarus and sitting bolt upright to deliver my own comprehensive medical opinion.

Since this amounted to, "I want to go home," she clearly preferred her own diagnosis. I could not, she asserted, redecorate the bedroom with a three-pint fountain of blood (royal Welsh variety) and expect early parole from hospital.

The prospect of a prolonged stay appalled me. Neither was I cheered by a visiting friend who said: "Well, you always wanted to look like Rock Hudson and now you do." A bit of a cheek coming from someone whose gentlest smile frightens horses and small children.

My immediate problem though, was how to fill in those interminable days which began at 6 am when the nurses woke us up so that we might nod off again for a couple of hours.

My thoughts refused to be marshalled sufficiently to allow me to write anything. My torpor was such that attempts at sustained reading induced deep sleep, disturbed only by people searching for a patch of virgin skin in which to jab yet another hypodermic.

Then I discovered the diverting down-market lonely hearts club whose members lonely, mercenary and plain old randy, prospect for potential partners or victims in the Personal columns of local newspapers.

How's this for a subtle and touchingly feminine approach to future happiness: "Attractive lady, 45, seeks man to spend money on her for fun. Age and looks not important." The fast cat might well have added, "Copy of bank statement appreciated."

Elsewhere, a patently shy woman who coyly described herself as being sexy and attractive was seeking a generous, home-owning gentleman of means. How askew Cupid's aim, his shafts now directed at wallets rather than the cardiac muscle's softer regions.

There was something arrogant and basic about the scarcely disguised aim of the slim male, 38, who was travelling to the South of France for June in a prestigious and comfortable car. Just a hint of snobbery attached to the bait.

Somewhat imperiously, he offered an attractive female in the 22 to 36 age range "the chance to share golden beaches and balmy nights" with a Riviera sun tan thrown in. It is highly unlikely that he was seeking a Miss Virginity contestant.

"I am tall, dark, handsome and 21 years old with a good job and a car," wrote another shrinking violet. Then why the need to advertise?

Perhaps the answer lay in his last line: "All I need is a nice young lady with a caring nature." Don't we all, son. I know men who would sacrifice a limb for such a prize.

Also looking for a rarity was the good-looking 35-year-old man who asked, "Is there a slim, good-looking, well educated, non-manic depressive female with a good sense of humour reading this?"

If there was, she can only have been doing it for entertainment value. Anyone with such attributes is unlikely to have been available to an off-the-peg stranger, despite the glowing report he gave himself.

There was a surprising preponderance of hopefuls looking for tall, non-smokers. Nothing wrong in that, except that it ruled out about 85 per cent of the population including me, who can only boast of being a handy size for carrying under the arm.

I imagine the photograph test must be quite unnerving and calculated to fragment already fragile egos if the portrait brings a negative response. It is also unfair, highly subjective and a most unreliable indicator of a person's character.

You can look like the product of a traffic accident and still be a better companion than your average Narcissus. And I speak for all of us in that category.

Few advertisers described themselves as being anything less than attractive, which betrays either vanity or insecurity. I suspect the latter because of the anonymity afforded by fishing in the dark for partners obliged to make the first positive move.

The bottom line is that there are a lot of lonely people out there willing to submit themselves to the embarrassment of having their pictures scanned and risking rejection. It's a hell of a way to find happiness, but good luck to them.

5 November, 1986

Pardon me, and blame it all on the Welsh

"FLIPPING HECK" (or words to that effect) I said to myself. "This calls for drastic action -something incisive, such as a letter to The Times." Since it was that august organ which had got up my nose, what better course of action to take?

What blocked my nostrils was that in his synopsis of Kingsley Amis's Booker Prize novel, the Literary Editor described it as being about "the awfulness of the Welsh." With a single bound I was into the saddle of my high horse.

"The casual denigration of an entire nation . . .," I began. "Unless this man has been reading my mail or talking to my wife, how can he possibly know that I am awful?" Soon I was in full petulant flow, bombarding the editor with little acid asides.

Did they have separate dining and toilet facilities for Welsh employees, I wanted to know. Since I was married to an Englishwoman, did this mean that the Literary Editor would look on my children as the progeny of a mixed marriage?

In short, I had a jolly good rant, realised I was being ridiculous, but felt a great deal better for letting off steam. I had been in grave danger of contributing to the lunacy which keeps the race relations industry afloat.

I still think that, in the interests of accuracy alone, The Times writer should have his legs smacked. You have to be fairly narrow-minded to believe that any race can be characterised by one of more traits and even sillier to propound the view in public.

My wife grew up believing there was something not quite nice about us little Celts and for years claimed she was intimidated by my odd sense of humour. Even today I sense she is only half-joking when she tries to explain some remark of mine by saying, "Take no notice. He's Welsh, y'know."

I shan't be reporting the cheeky madam to anyone, but I am going to have to watch my mouth after mildly shocking some lovely young thing who is not used to my ways. It made me realise how the company of journalists has divorced me from the attitudes of others.

Anyone stumbling unaware into my circle could be forgiven for thinking they had disturbed a nest of warring vipers rather than a group of close friends. There is no shortage of wit, but some of it can be quite murderous. It helps to get one's retaliation in first.

It was a colleague who, tired of a woman's remarks about his appearance, said "Thank you for sparing a thought for my problems when you could be so fully occupied with your own." She was never heard to criticise him again.

Another colleague, who lives in the country, sometimes wore a heavy tweed ensemble which became known as his Young Farmers' Club suit. He wearied of being asked how he had got on in the ploughing match or the hedging competition and all the other jokes associated with pastoral life. The suit has not been seen since.

A friend who suffered a minor nervous breakdown would sometimes suffer bouts of melancholia after his discharge. "Look at me," he moaned one day. "A bloody nutter who's been in a loony bin." I positively exploded. "Don't dare talk like that. You had a minor breakdown and spent ten days in a small clinic within a proper hospital. There is nothing wrong with you."

He thanked me for talking sense and said he should listen to me more often, just as I should listen to him about my problems. "You must be joking," I replied. "Listen to some bloody nutter who's been in a loony bin?" His little black cloud was swept away by a gale of laughter. Others might have cried, but he's used to me after all these years.

So is the probation officer who sometimes cooks dinner for us and has never been allowed to forget the night blood spurted out of our underdone chicken portions. Recently he was seriously thinking of changing jobs and applying to become assistant governor at The Maze Prison in Belfast. I gave him a real earful about the dangers he and his family would face and told him not to be daft.

Well, he said, a businessman had offered to set him up in a restaurant, with him doing all the cooking. "Take The Maze job, take The Maze job," I pleaded in mock horror and he knew I was thinking of the chicken again. He nearly choked on his beer.

The trouble is, I think in those terms all the time, never allowing a serious thought to enter my head if one can be avoided. It's joking off the cuff which sometimes gets me into trouble since my brain is rarely engaged at the same time. I'm lucky not to have been smacked in the mouth a few times.

There have been lots of frosty glances, some rude words and, only on Saturday, a stiff-fingered dig in the ribs from a guest who misinterpreted something I said to my long-suffering wife.

Out came the explanation of my ethnic origins by way of excuse and the bit about the Welsh being gourmets at the feast of insults. Maybe I shall report her, after all.

l March, 1989

Everybody loves a loser, know what I mean, Harry

NOW IT'S official. We can all feel free to admire, love and respect Frank Bruno because he stayed on his feet for approximately 14 minutes while Mike Tyson beat several different substances out of him.

This signal honour was conferred upon us by Harry Carpenter, seasoned commentator, dropper of memorable goolies and an absolute gift to students of comic prophecies.

"He's done us proud. All the world will now have respect for him," Harry said after the referee stepped in to save our hero from having his brains irreparably scrambled by an uncontrollable, vicious threshing machine.

This was a rather large assumption since, generally speaking, the world reserves its admiration for winners. Long gone are the days when merely taking part was enough. Now you have to be the top of the heap.

As far as I can determine, ours is the only nation which applauds failure and, in effect, says, "Didn't he lose well?" It is an endearing trait which must be of great comfort to all our "nearly" sportsmen and women.

If we view the big fight dispassionately, we see Bruno being dumped on the canvas within seconds, losing every round and then being rescued from fearful punishment before the contest had reached the halfway stage.

Bruno landed only two significant blows, at which point Harry howled, "Go after him, Frank." So much for the BBC's much-vaunted impartiality. Given the cold facts, I am at a loss to understand the euphoria surrounding such a decisive defeat.

The man's courage is unquestionable and he certainly did better than some of the other gladiators dispatched by the Neanderthal look-alike. But, in pursuit of £1m, he was comprehensively outclassed and well beaten.

Even allowing for the adjectival excesses of some sports writers, big Frank's status as a hero eludes me. Harry reckoned Americans would also have new respect for him. It is more likely that in a country where winning is all, they will merely be less contemptuous of his abilities.

Anyone who remembers Tommy Farr will probably do so for one reason. Not for the fact that he distinguished himself in the British ring, but because he lost to that supreme champion, Joe Louis.

There is similar nostalgia for Don Cockell because he took such a dreadful pummelling from Rocky Marciano and lost very bravely. And anyone interested in boxing will recall Bruce Woodcock's glorious defeat at the hands of an American who broke his jaw.

Who among tennis fans can ever forget the exquisite agony they were put through by Virginia Wade? It was almost an annual event. She so perfected the art of losing she was a national heroine long before she became careless and actually won at Wimbledon.

Remember, too, how Roger Taylor was lionised, though I suspect it was more for his dark good looks than how he wielded a racket. He was practically deified when he reached the semi-finals of the men's singles and lived up to expectations by exiting with pride, but no prize.

Latterly, after a string of dismal failures which proved too much even for the British, Sue Barker was supplanted in the public's affections by Annabel Croft. God knows why, because she always played like a big girl's blouse.

While admirably consistent in losing, she sensed she was not doing it in a style which would put her in the Wade class. Astutely she quit while she was well behind and, unaccountably, was rewarded with a contract to be the surrogate rear of Anneka Rice in Treasure Hunt.

In winter sports we have a failure of international renown in Eddie "The Eagle" Edwards for all his pluck in attempting the skiing equivalent of the high and long jumps, he was a gross embarrassment to everyone except himself and the Canadians.

The Canadians understand failure. Living next door to the USA and dominated by its dreadful television output and ugly cars, they have a national inferiority complex of Brobdingnagian proportions.

Eddie acquired celebrity status, frequently appears on TV and makes public appearances - when he is not busy breaking his collar bone. In which other country, I ask you, could someone succeed matriculating in inefficacy?

There are exceptions. The Welsh do not recognise failure. On hearing the latest score from Cardiff Arms Park or Twickers, they send their TV sets for repair rather than believe the national side is losing.

No English cricket captain ever became a hero through defeat, no matter how narrow the margin. It's their game, they taught it to the world and no side made up of Antipodean ockers or dusky colonials has any business winning against them.

Normally, though, we love a jolly good loser. That is why Bruno is now basking in the peculiarly British sunshine of defeat.

6 September, 1989

The process of growing old disgracefully

I HAVE never shared the view that getting old entitles anyone to anything, unless it's a degree of care when they are unable to look after themselves. But you would do that for your fellow man anyway at whatever age.

Some cultures venerate their elders in the belief that longevity confers upon them a wisdom and experience to be almost hallowed. Not so. Someone who is stupid and crotchety at 20 is unlikely to be improved by approaching senility.

In fact, old age is often used to excuse a multitude of sins. People are generally more tolerant of ill-mannered septuagenarians than ever they would be of a teenager. There is no difference between them except a few decades.

It's just that, in the case of the elderly, people are more inclined to say, "You'll be old yourself one day." Sometimes age does account for aberrations, but there are an awful lot of people who play on the number of summers they have seen.

These thoughts crossed my mind when I was trapped in the pub by one of the most opinionated and obnoxious men it has ever been my misfortune to meet. Into the bargain he was plainly quite thick.

He belonged to that school of pensioners who reach 65 and suddenly discover that their income is inadequate. No matter that they have had a lifetime to consider this eventuality, they are still surprised.

They pick up their pens and write angry letters to the local newspapers. They become political animals who identify the Government as the villain of the piece. It doesn't matter which government.

All their lives they have lived with the knowledge that whichever party has been in power, the old age pension has not been enough to keep anyone in aniseed balls for a week. Sixty-five years is a long time for a penny to drop.

Anyway, this man, who spent a lot of time draining his frugal resources down the pub toilet, had become educated. Without prompting, he was able to tell me in detail how much better off were his counterparts in Europe.

I suggested that, now Britain was such a committed member of the EC, he might consider moving house. I omitted to mention that this would be mostly for my benefit, but the subtlety was lost on him in any case.

"It's that bloody Thatcher woman," he said. I was moved to point out that, although insufficient, the pension rate has never been higher. With stunning logic he replied, "She's a right cow."

He then launched into the "I fought for my country" speech followed by the set piece about, "I never took a day off work unless I was really ill." Admirable, except that he now seems to think the world owes him a living.

It doesn't. His mind has been put to sleep by the welfare state, which has bred the indolent mentality that anything wrong with his life can be righted by a civil servant with a row of ball-point pens in his breast pocket.

People have become too lazy to think or do for themselves. So they write to newspapers to complain how badly done by they are. They know how small is the pension, but wait 65 years before becoming vociferous grey panthers.

They wear penury like a badge. They push children to one side and complain about the behaviour of the young. They jump queues with their free bus passes and, if you're lucky they say, "Excuse me, I'm a pensioner." So what?

We all need to get home, we've stood in the rain just as long and have to pay for the privilege of being shaken about while standing all the way to one's destination. I readily defer to age, but only if it is possessed of intelligence and manners.

Both those qualities are now rarities in people of all ages. This is the age of the crude and the coarse. Only last week I got off a bus two stops early because of the Scotland Road women who were freely using four-letter words in front of their bairns.

It is difficult to imagine that they will improve with age but, no doubt, when they are in receipt of a pension they will be vainly trying to claim the immunity from life's vagaries that seniority is mistakenly supposed to bring.

It doesn't. You stop working, but remain the same person. If you're cunning, you methodically play on the fact that you are retired and deserve preferential treatment to which you are not entitled.

If you are sensible and prudent, you look ahead and spend as much as possible on a private pension plan which will allow you to live more or less in the manner to which you are accustomed.

In this way you save on postage and stationery by not having to write ireful letters about Mrs Thatcher and feel no need to bore total strangers to death in the pub.

You simply grow up and realise that once your working life is over, no-one is going to keep you in beer and fags. If you do not make provision for that eventuality, then you will simply have to give up booze and tobacco.

No government of any political shade is ever going to give you what you really want, which is total reliance on the state because you've been too idle, spendthrift or parsimonious to do anything for yourself.

It's worth thinking about, if only because it might prevent you from becoming the pub bore.

10 August, 1988

Lets give this silly art a skip

SOME years ago, I literally quick-stepped with glee when first prize in the John Moores Exhibition was awarded to a totally white canvas. Its title escapes me now, but it could well have been "Interior of a Snowdrift."

It had all the features of the blank sheets of paper I feed into my typewriter, which have no artistic merit even when I have defiled their virginity. My own theory was that the painter had the cheek of two Pucks and was trying to extract some liquid from the art establishment.

That he succeeded seemed to present a wonderful opportunity for our then arts editor to draw his sword and puncture a few pretension-filled paunches. He demurred and said, "It's not just white, you know, it's different shades of white." Because of his Scottish roots I promptly dubbed him McJude the Obscure.

Since my own efforts with a brush often produce variegations of the same colour I'm thinking seriously of submitting a bathroom wall for next year's competition.

This memory sprang back when I read about the esteemed panel of judges at the New York Chair Fair weighing the merits of entries in the Ad Hoc Avantgarde Chair section. Subtle comparisons and rarefied discussion led them to choose the work of Mr Tom Musorafita.

His name was unknown to the distinguished audience, and small wonder. He was a construction worker on the unfinished design centre. When he saw the entries arriving he decided, as a joke, to make a seat from the leftovers in his skip. He simply nailed together a cardboard drum, a piece of plasterboard and a green plastic lid.

"I can't believe this piece of garbage won anything," said the award-winning craftsman. "I had to look up 'ad hoc' to make sure they weren't yanking me around." As with the white canvas, art was perceived where it did not exist.

We have had the infamous pile of bricks and the heap of coal. Now Liverpool has that most brilliant piece of conceptual inspiration - the glass of water masquerading as an oak tree. Can we assume that when some of the water evaporates it cleverly transforms itself into an example of bonsai.

Modern art being what it is - the product of highly individualistic thought - we must concede that when the sculptor creatively turned on the tap to fill the tumbler he really did perceive the birth of an oak tree. Too few of us are blessed with that kind of vision.

But if he says it is a tree, then that is what it is. By the same token, we might look at it and see something completely different - such as a small and neat, yet distinctive pile of bull droppings. Alternatively, it might appear to us to be a glass of water with its acorns missings.

What blocks my nostrils is the velvet jacket brigade who pretend they can climb inside the artist's head and share his cerebral experience.

I recall the grand televised opening of the Tate when into camera ambled what looked like a Kodiak bear en route to a barbecue. In fact, it was art critic Adrian Henri who had been lumbered with the awesome task of describing a series of canvases depicting random dark stripes on uniformly burgundy backgrounds.

They were not unpleasing to the eye, but what to make of them? Adrian almost broke into a walk in his haste to escape an embarrassing moment. He did utter a few words, but ended up saying nothing.

I am not impervious to the appeal of modern art. I could happily live with the odd Mondrian, Braque or Modigliani. I would even accept one of those Picasso women with one eye and three breasts (or is it the other way around?) but only for monetary reasons.

Womaniser that he was, I doubt whether Pablo actually met such an unfortunate being except in his mind. Or was it a nightmare? For some expert to wax lyrical about a grotesque vision depicted with erratic draughtsmanship is laughable. Only Picasso really understood what he was trying to say.

I think the Tate has been taken. Whoever chose the more outlandish exhibits has obviously turned Pseuds Corner and is well on the way to the funny farm. Either that, or they are simply afraid to stare a glass of water in the eye and say, "I see no tree."

If ever a monarch again strides out in the nude and invites the cheering masses to admire his new clothes, let us hope there will still be an innocent little boy to step from the crowd and point out that the king is starkers.

25 January, 1989

Howzat! Well, in my view, it's puerility

WHEN LAST I checked up, cricket was still a game requiring ten bits of wood, 22 players, two bats and a ball. Although confusing for any emergent nation such as America, whose national sport is a glorified game of rounders, the relatively complex rules contain no embargo on foreign travel.

Participants are merely required to strike, bowl, throw or catch the ball in an effort to score, or prevent the scoring of runs. Although it is no more than a usually boring leisure pursuit, England employs a national team whose apparent role is to notch up fewer runs than any other country's side.

This they do particularly well and it is one of the peculiarities of this largely lethargic pastime that its players receive handsome sums of money, bottles of champagne and lucrative advertising contracts for losing spectacularly.

Another odd facet is that the man chosen to lead the team is remembered for the rest of his life, and often beyond his demise, as someone adjudged to have the wisdom of Solomon and the tactical skills of Field Marshall Montgomery, despite an embarrassing series of failures.

Players are spoken of in reverential tones in some holy place called the Long Room by moustachioed old duffers who firmly believe that all that is best about England is embodied in the straightness of a man's bat.

It should at this point be remembered that we are mulling over nothing of greater gravitas than a ball game. Or, at least, that is what it used to be before the world's rumbling, bumbling, pompously moralising hypocrites got their knickers in the most convoluted twist.

Although Britain is notionally part of the free world, that stuffy lot otherwise known as the Test and County Cricket Board are supporting moves calculated to harm or hinder individual lives.

The grave "crime" at issue is that of playing professionally with a ball in South Africa, and yesterday the International Cricket Conference decided to ban from international matches any player with sporting contacts with South Africa for three, four or five years, depending on the contract.

After a great deal of thought, the only parallel I can think of is the puerile spite with which my children squabble over the ownership of their dolls. Except, of course, that this business has far more sinister implications for the subjects of a shameful witch-hunt.

It is every bit as shabby and vicious as McCarthyism. The fundamental rights of individuals to travel and pursue their careers are in danger of being negated by people with minds scarcely the size of peanuts.

How ironic that those they so maliciously seek to penalise are the very sportsmen who coach and play cricket with young blacks. The angry brigade are actually discriminating against the people they so piously profess to care about.

Yes, apartheid is abhorrent and, yes, the sadistic South African police are known for sending prisoners on unscheduled flights from high windows. Afrikaaner politics could do with a dose of Domestos, but you won't cleanse them by depriving an Englishman of his living.

I wonder, too, about the altruism of the holier-than-thou gang who vilified, threatened and virtually ran out of Britain a little girl for no better reason than that she was born in South Africa. Zola Budd found another version of apartheid in this sceptred isle.

Where were these noisy empty vessels when the England cricket team was captained by Tony Greig, or when Mike Proctor was a leading county player? How still their voices when Frank Bruno fought Gerry Coetzee?

Other cricketing countries have wisely and carefully exempted themselves from any form of censure. India for instance, refused to play an English team which included men who had played in South Africa.

Meantime, it happily continued with its own contemptuous brand of discrimination against the so-called "untouchables" because of the loathsome caste system. How India can strike such a moralistic pose against South Africa and justify the abysmal treatment of their own people is beyond me.

No athlete who ever competed in any of these countries has been threatened with the loss of his career - or earnings. Quite right, too. Since politics is such a dirty and duplicitous business, we should at least try to keep sport clean.

The notion that the world can be changed by seriously damaging the life of someone who knocks a ball about is too absurd for words. As I said, it is only a ball game.

28 September, 1988

Extending my parameters at the Tate ...

I HAVE a notion that Richard Francis, curator of the Tate Gallery, thinks me awfully plebeian. It must be something to do with his having said that I was ignorant. He is nothing if not direct - but in the most urbane manner.

Mr Francis was kindly trying to remedy the situation by giving me a quick arts appreciation course. He had read my recent criticisms of some of the more obscure works to have been seen there.

Even with his expert guidance, I doubt that I would ever have been able to look at that now famous glass of water and see an oak tree. However, that particular treasure has now moved on to be marvelled at elsewhere. It will surely be missed by Liverpool's silviculturists.

There are, however, other works to mystify the untutored and the ignorant. I am so retarded that I gazed at what appeared to be a notice board without realising that it was a notable work by an artist "extending the parameters of sculpture."

The piece was called "Two straight twelve-mile walks over Dartmoor" and bore two lists of words. Mostly they were the names of landmarks en route with occasional references to the conditions, e.g. "darkness", "creak of ice."

Mr Francis, plainly getting a bit cheesed off by now, was adamant that it was a work of art. It put me in mind of similar pieces of sculpture just inside the gates of all public parks.

We also had a minor disagreement over another exhibit by two blokes who apparently see all of life as a work of art. To capture just one aspect they photographed each other drinking in a pub. The pictures- about 40 of them - are all of abysmal quality and composition with several totally out of focus.

I expressed the opinion that this particular sculpture must surely be a joke. The flicker of pain which crossed my guide's face stopped me from asking about the artistic merits of a nearby old and dirty washing machine which sported a gaping hole in its body.

However, even with my scant knowledge, I was able to identify it as belonging to the now obsolete school of early Hotpoint. Perhaps that is what it was trying tell me.

Elsewhere in the gallery there was an excellent exhibition of surrealist paintings, only a few of which defeated me. Mr Francis lauded Birth by Jackson Pollock, but to my coarse eye it looked like a hearty breakfast which had been put through a blender.

I cared little for Mirot's work and it's "language of symbols and sexuality," but was much taken by most else in a collection which constitutes a history of the surreal movement. There's some powerful stuff on show.

The Rothko Room, with its huge burgundy canvases bearing featureless blocks of other colours, remains a mystery to me. "It has to be taken on a great deal of trust by the first-time viewer," Mr Francis said. I'll go along with that.

He granted that it was not easy to either interpret or explain. He felt it to have a meditative quality. One needed to sit and think to try to work it out, but he thought he could detect Rothko's sense of foreboding and despair about the 20th century.

At his bidding I stood very close to one painting, completely filling my vision in order to see whether the colours would move for me as they had for him. We philistines have no luck. They didn't budge an inch.

I obviously flunked the course, but picked up some smashing phrases with which to mask my ignorance - a word which Mr Francis was kind enough to define for me. It was a morning full of learning and, were it not for the nagging memory of that old washing machine, I would feel a much better man.

15 August, 1982

It's kick-off time for cretins

WHAT A depressing thought that all over Britain earnest young men are probably filing the edges of bicycle chains, weighing their cudgels and honing their darts.

The more dedicated might even be putting in a couple of hours' practice at ripping upholstery, breaking toilets and smashing windows. It is even conceivable that there are group training sessions for those a little rusty in the techniques of jostling old ladies and terrorising whole towns.

Yes, after a summer of comparative sanity the open season for hooliganism is once more upon us. When the first referee sounds his whistle on that fateful Saturday - August 18 - it will be kick-off time for cretins.

The really dreary thing about a long and discontenting winter of soccer is that it is all so predictable, from the antics of the dolts on the terraces through to the lower half of one's TV screen being occupied by Jimmy Hill's chin.

No uncanny vision is needed to know that magistrates will hand out stern warnings and totally inadequate fines to those engaged in orchestrated aggro.

Commentators will once again confer genius and other unwarranted attributes on very ordinary young men with the arrogance of Greek gods and the vocabularies of four-year-olds.

Commentator: "Well, Bobby, what a magnificent goal."

Bobby: "Yeah, David, magic."

Commentator: "It must have been a great feeling to score at such a crucial time in the match."

Bobby: "Well, yeah, I couldn't believe it reely. Magic, y'know."

Commentator: "Here it is again in replay. Would you like to take us through it?"

Bobby: "Well, y'know, Jimmy collected the ball on the right. 'Ee was magic to-day, y'know. 'Ee beat 'is man, y'know, and slipped it inside to me. Reel magic, y'know. I saw their sweeper out of the corner of me eye, y'know, and slipped it through 'is legs, y'know. Then their goalie came but I just 'it it, y'know. Magic."

Commentator: "Thanks, Bobby. And good luck to the lads in the third round second-leg replay of the European Cup Winners' Cup play-off in the Eastern Zone finals."

Bobby: "Magic, David."

Commentators seem to fare better than mere sports writers, who apparently have to kowtow and pay not inconsiderable sums of money to register each cough and hiccup of ball-kickers with an acumen belied by the banality of their utterances.

Still with a fortitude born of a real need to pay the mortgage and household bills, they will continue to invent cliches eulogising leg movements which are commonplace on each Saturday throughout the season.

How long before we read: "Domehead in shock move bid?" This means that the petulant "star" has been dropped for one match and feels sorely aggrieved, or is not satisfied with £300 a week and wants to leave.

And how long before the first manager, saddled with a team of Greek gods who can't put the ball in the net, is cruelly dumped in the dole queue by a chairman who probably did not even aspire to rounders at school?

This will surely be followed by a manager lobbing out £2,000,000 for a striker who will inevitably fail to strike, but whose meanderings in midfield will be described as intelligent by a TV pundit. "He may not have scored, but he's a great player off the ball," someone is bound to say.

Then there will be the endless analyses, replays and slow-motion playbacks of J. Hill and Chin. Followed by Goal of the Month, Save of the Week and Foul of the Year.

On the pitch there will be the usual display of full frontal kissing after each goal and the classic gesture of innocence from defenders, fed on raw meat all week, after kicking an opponent in the air or ending his career.

This Theatre of the Absurd takes on a whole new dimension when England meet the Italians or South Americans, noted for their deadly accurate spitting and blocking techniques, which would have done credit to Attila the Hun.

And talking of sportsmen, who does not live in dread of a visit from Scottish supporters? The mere announcement of their impending arrival is enough to close most bars and shops lest a year's industry is ground to dust by these loyal fans.

Ah yes, the football season is here again. Are you ready for it? Magic.

15 August, 1990

It's the luck of the Irish to suffer our prejudices

A FEW years ago, while week-ending in bubblin' Dublin, I went out for dinner and for my main course ordered half a spring chicken. And that, sited in splendid isolation in the middle of a large plate, was exactly what I got.

No greens, no potatoes. Just the bisected fowl, done to death before owning its first pair of long trousers. A gentle word with the literally minded waitress soon won the bird some company on the platter.

Later, lying abed, I began to read an article in the airline's ultra glossy magazine. It was prefaced with a note saying that some pages had been printed out of sequence and if I wanted to read them in the correct order etc . . .

But it seemed like too much hassle and as I reflected on the evening the beginning of a smile arrived simultaneously with the thought: How very Irish. And how remiss of me to have so carelessly embraced invidious stereotyping.

Just let the word "Irishman" percolate through your mind and see what adjectives are thrown out. More than likely they will be drunken, stupid, aggressive and rebellious. We do them a grave injustice.

It is largely forgotten - if it were ever known - that their tiny population has turned out a surprising number of scholars and men of letters. We also overlook the fact that per head of population, they read more newspapers than any nation in Europe.

Yet, they are still thought of as thick Micks. It is part of a long-established prejudice far more complex than the bias we harbour against coloured ethnic groups simply because they are glaringly different in appearance.

An Irishman in Britain can walk the streets unnoticed until he opens his mouth. Then he is automatically compartmentalised and shoved back into the filing system which is home to our hasty and injurious judgments.

These go back many years, long before the mass migrations sparked by the famines of the 18th century. They continue today, now cruelly compounded by the actions of the gangsters and murderers of the IRA.

I once tried to persuade the committee of Liverpool's Irish Centre to let me talk to them after the next atrocity so that I could gauge the impact on their community. In that way, I said, we might be able to eradicate a lot of misunderstandings. The idea appeared to have found favour but, despite my efforts, petered out. It became clear that the Irish community suffering guilt by association preferred to keep a low profile.

Past IRA actions had caused them some aggro, including violence when their accents had been heard in certain pubs. That's as silly as beating up Welshmen because some nit set fire to a holiday home in Snowdonia.

Between outrages, they go about their business sotto voce and things settle down. Then comes something horrific like the murder of Ian Gow and they are back living on pins and needles.

In several parts of Britain they live in constant fear of being picked up under the Prevention of Terrorism Act often merely for the "crime" of having an Irish accent. This can ruin careers even if, as in the case of the vast majority, they are released without being charged.

The nightmarish injustices which befell the Guildford Four are still fresh in their minds. As someone wrote recently, England takes the Irish to its bosom, the better to get a purchase on their throats.

After Gow's death I asked a man in a Liverpool pub how he felt about the inevitable tide of resentment which would follow. "We are not all thugs and killers. We are just as horrified as a nation by the actions of the IRA as the people in Britain are.

"Simply to tar us all with the same brush is both ignorant and demeaning." I believe him, especially after seeing IRA fund collectors being spurned on the streets of Dublin.

Another woman said that each atrocity made her feel visible as soon as she opened her mouth. "I wish the IRA would stop. It makes life difficult and I'm not into what they do anyway. They're just a shower of nuts."

Badly abused on the labour market, especially the construction industry, they tread a line between paranoia and despair and fear sinking into the sort of social oblivion that has taken so many of their countrymen before them.

With our histories for so long intertwined, you'd think by now that a measure of understanding would have been achieved. We sadly underestimate our capacity for irrational bigotry. What a shame.

4 May, 1988

A sorry lament from one small boy of 50

THE GILDED, sweet bird of youth long ago flew my coop. Last week it dispatched one of its avian kin to briefly settle on my window sill and make derisory noises about my needing a new embalmer. It was an albatross and it was my 50th birthday.

Insensitive folk asked how it felt, as if I had just undergone an operation in readiness for an inspection by Arthur Negus, were he still alive. Since I have a Master's in Lethargy, there are those who think Arthur and I now have much in common.

The feeling was much the same as on the day I noisily emerged from the womb. One of vulnerability, a need for swaddling and coddling, plenty of support for the head and some liquid sustenance.

When you have mislaid the greater part of your life, including some vintage golden years, the certain knowledge that it will never turn up in the Lost and Found department is a mite sobering. That's how the big Five-0 clobbers you.

I might have borne the mid-life crisis with greater fortitude had not the woman who introduced me to the bliss of human bondage (without the aid of velvet chains) announced that she was leaving at the end of this week.

"Do you mind if I go?" she asked with all the confidence of one expecting to be offered a lift in a tumbril. Stretching to my full height (a short exercise), I did a passable impression of Gielgud as Elizabeth Barratt Browning's wickedly austere dad.

"You are over 21 and can do as you please without my permission," I replied. To make things easier for her, I added, "If you wish to desert me and the children that is entirely your decision." I was splendidly huffy.

Disconcertingly, she began to look happy. So to further boost her optimism I pitched in with, "The only thing that worries me where you are going to live when, and if, you return. There'll be no place for you here."

Her smile would have warmed a winter's frost. "Very good, chucky, but they gave you away again," she said, as if addressing a small boy which, give or take a few years, is what I am.

By "they" she meant my nostrils, which always flare when I attempt to deceive. My face can be rigid as a poker, but the old spiracles belong on the smug face of a matador arrogantly strutting his stuff on a blood-soaked stage of sand.

So it is that, on Saturday Mrs W and her luggage will pass through the front door bound for some far-flung foreign outpost not to be seen again for an eternity. Since, on this occasion, she will be carrying her own cases it will be interesting to see if she leaves behind any of the heavier items of kitchen furniture.

By an eternity I mean four or five days on a freebie visit to Portugal, during which I shall have to be my own chatelaine, child-minder and dresser, bed-maker and cook. Even now I am calculating what four consecutive suppers of egg and chips will do to my little ones' cholesterol levels.

I think I can cope with the housekeeping problems by inviting friendly vandals to break in and tidy the place up on the eve of my wife's return. It's sure to be a mess. The big problem will be drumming the concept of the passage of time into the children's heads.

They will be expecting their mother home in time for tea. Thereafter there will be half-hourly queries about her ETA back in England which, as the days pass, will give way to whining and pining.

Against all the odds, this will be the first time my wife has left me. Being 50 is somehow supposed to confer on me a mellowness and maturity which comes out of the mouth as, "You go, love. Enjoy yourself. You'd be silly to turn it down." Echoing around the walls of a churning stomach is the scream, "Don't go. For pity's sake don't go."

Neither does age confer wisdom, only the knowledge that life is a series of crises punctuated by moments of tranquillity. As Terry Wogan was fond of saying, there's not one door that shuts but than another slams in your face. Have you seen the state of my nose?

The half-century, a dismal milestone, also seems to induce a futile streak of vanity manifested in a desire to leave some kind of mark, no matter how small, on the world. Now that the wheel has been invented, the atom split and brains transplanted, there's not a lot left.

So, hopefully with my wife's participation, I have decided to try for another baby before I become totally addled. The new little Williams will fill the void when the other two eventually emigrate to Palermo to attain their goal of becoming fully-fledge *mafiosi* .

A friend told me not to be so solemn about my age. I would, he assured me, assume the aura of a seasoned sugar daddy and be pursued by nubile young things in gymslips. So far, I've been followed by a couple of friendly dogs.

I know how to be a daddy, but all my sugar is swallowed by the bank and the building society. What care I? Age, give or take the odd creaking joint, is but a state of mind - and my mind has always been in a right old state.

28 March, 1990

Rich coming from Gucci left-wingers

I AM as politically aware today as I was on that April morning in 1940 when I poked my head from the womb and decided that the placenta was a better place to be. Life's inexorable cycle dictated that I should join its wayward games.

Long have I striven to distance myself from the norm in the unflagging belief that oddballs have far more common sense than the logicians slavishly bound by ideologies. There is little to choose between egomaniacs of any persuasion.

I recall that at about the age of twelve I asked my mother why she voted Labour. "Because Dad does," she replied. This did not seem to me a compelling reason since his view of global politics was governed by the amount of duty he paid on fags, booze and petrol.

He also laboured under the misapprehension that socialists existed solely to better his lot because he belonged to that near-extinct breed known as the working man. He could never grasp that Paul Getty toiling 18 hours a day, seven days a week, fell into the same category.

The only differences were their wage packets and aspirations. One assiduously trod in the footsteps of Croesus while the other was happy to live in a council house and conform to the Labour stereotype, although he eschewed the cloth cap, whippet in tow and a passion for pigeons.

Incredibly, though, that image still exists. I never tire of recalling how Tony Benn used to entertain trades union tyrants with mugs of tea and bacon butties blissfully unaware that they were more accustomed to being chauffeur-driven to the Savoy for lunch.

The worst thing that ever happened to socialism was when it was embraced by caring, liberal capitalists sipping champagne while empathising the plight of their mild and bitter fellows.

There was something sick about the owners - some of them in the Labour Cabinet - of two or three homes opposing the sale of council houses. Similarly, it was ridiculous for the likes of Harold Pinter, Lady Antonia Fraser, John Mortimer and friends, all beneficiaries of the capitalist system, to form a precious coterie of Bollinger Bolsheviks.

Little do they know, in a country riven by the politics of envy, how much they are despised by those who are conspicuously absent from their pretentiously intellectual discursions on an ideology beset by *rigor mortis*.

Last week I was discussing books with the lady who comes to clean our house. I commended to her Children of the Rich by William Davis, and commented on the fact that many of its subjects had led lives bedevilled by great misfortune.

She laughed and said, "Oh that's all right then." It reminded me that Britain is still one of those countries in which wealth is regarded as a crime. To do well is to transgress, to own that which others want but have not the *nous* or drive to work for.

When crooner Tom Jones goes home to South Wales he no longer drinks with his old mates. If he buys a round he is accused of flashing his money. If he does not, he is condemned for being mean.

Although it is well within his means, DJ David Hamilton would never buy a Rolls-Royce because of the vandalism its symbolism would attract.

Calls for a fairer distribution of wealth usually mean: "You've got more than me and I don't like it." Even the intelligent Denis Healey the worst Chancellor we've ever had, succumbed to class envy when he jubilantly threatened to "squeeze the rich until their pips squeak."

What is so wrong about having money? Do not many of us aspire to wealth every time we fill in a football coupon or buy a Premium Bond? Why should the improbability of winning make us social lepers to be punitively caned by adherents of a dead credo?

However, it is clearly time for Mrs Thatcher to go. Her unfettered power seems to have created a sense of omnipotence and delusions of unfailing adequacy. Like all politicians, she has committed the cardinal sin of failing to listen to those who presented her with a mandate.

The poll tax is merely one manifestation of her apparent deafness. Another was her reaction to the embarrassment of the Mid-Staffs by-election which revealed a streak of unbelievable obduracy. Even her own rank and file members have now realised that no matter how high the asbestos content of her underwear, Mrs T is no longer fireproof. They have tired of her patronising "Nanny knows best" philosophy.

She's on her way out which would be fine for the country if only there was an acceptable alternative. There seems little point in exchanging one inflexible dogma for another or, even worse, voting for Paddy Ashdown's party of invisible men. Unless you happen to be naive or terminally bewildered and believe that Neil Kinnock will create Nirvana in six days and negotiate a grossly inflated rate of overtime for the Sunday.

Anyone who thinks that the almost inevitable ascendancy of a Labour will make a shred of difference to their lives was probably born a few days ago. They should start looking for jobs now, because all ideologies cost money. Yours and mine.

11 January, 1989

The love that springs from hate eternal

SOMEONE in my position, lowly though it be, is bound to receive a fair percentage of hate mail. However, I shall not bore you with the prejudices of my family and friends.

Readers' letters, even those written in either red or green ink on lined paper, are always welcome. I still treasure those from the man who is furious with me for refusing to acknowledge the contribution of Rudolf Hess to Britain's war effort.

Then there was the anonymous correspondence (deliberately written in red to amuse and inflame me) from a man who hates Theatr Clwyd in Mold. I could only conclude that he had been deprived of a mother-in-law or had abusive parents.

Given that Mold was previously the sort of town where the family pig was put on a wall to watch a passing band march by, I would have thought the theatre was as welcome as a water hole in the Gobi desert.

There was also the woman who took exception to my observation that Victoria Principal's bosom jiggled as she walked. Her letter was extremely vituperative, but I thank her for the mammary.

Mail from literary snobs is common, though they always fail to appreciate that one's work can be distorted or influenced by other hands. Lofty grammarians, ignorant of newspaper production methods can also be a pain in the aspidistra.

Recently, for instance, I was castigated for the misspelling of "anathema." The word had passed before three pairs of expert eyes but appeared in print without the second vowel. The rapidity with which readers pounce on these errors never ceases to amaze me.

Most letters stem from emotion rather than logic. Those written in garish inks usually come from people whose main occupation is the idle contemplation of a spot of basket weaving. But they deserve their say.

As does the Bangor doctor who sent me a cutting of a Joan Bakewell article about the Welsh following her *Heart of the Matter* programme on television. It was a nice piece, bland, uncritical, partly obsequious, but nice.

Just what the doctor ordered. "What a difference between Joan Bakewell's sympathetic view and the bitter anti-Welsh script that you write," he said in a curt note. There was a big difference.

This column does not exist to pay homage to bombings, arson or the childish use of superglue in estate agents' offices. Ms Bakewell dwelt mainly on culture and the arts, neither of which can be reconciled with potentially fatal yobbism.

Though the Welsh language is important, not least because it is the oldest and arguably the purest tongue in Europe, it can also be beautiful and lyrical. But not when mixed with explosives.

You need to live and work in England to know what a grave disservice is done to Wales by the activists. You cannot with one hand accept foreign investment and, with the other, strike a match to set fire to your benefactors' homes.

Much as I respect Dafydd Iwan, vice-chairman of Plaid Cymru, I found quite outrageous his suggestion that there should be controls on the numbers of English people allowed to live in Welsh communities.

To my mind, that is apartheid and parochialism in extremis. In fact, it is also racist and illegal. Britain is supposed to be a free country and not a patchwork of ghettos for self-indulgent minorities.

If the same notion were to be embraced by other nations then the populations of Liverpool and Patagonia would be decimated overnight. The Welsh are everywhere, so how can they even entertain the idea of disbarring the English.

Even if Britain was not now a polyglot nation the idea would still be too silly for words. Isolationism in whatever form would ruin Wales at a stroke. Everybody needs good neighbours.

The good doctor also overlooked the fact that in her gushing piece Bakewell also mentioned Arts Council funding. That means British, not just Welsh, taxpayers' money. Theatr Clwyd could not exist without it.

I am not inordinately proud of being Welsh because I find the parameters of nationalism too confining. They are also dangerous when wired up to incendiary devices which, inexplicably, are meant to advance the cause of culture.My other mail seems to have stemmed mainly from a column about an "old time" gospel meeting at which the minister condemned all those who were not Presbyterian.

He also found the time to attribute a broken glass to the work of the devil and blamed all terminal diseases on evil living rather than malignant organisms. I thought he was talking mumbo-jumbo.

One of those who troubled to write said he spotted me as a sinner the moment I walked through the door. I have that kind of face, I am afraid. Even God-fearing Christians condemn me without knowing me.

Another suggested attending a special service for "people such as yourself." He said that God loves me, "though things will have to change." Such as what?

Readers are very judgemental, but I wouldn't have it any other way. Please keep the letters coming.

PEOPLE AND PLACES

PEOPLE always fascinated John and with his remarkable gift of perception he was able to understand them - sometimes better than they knew themselves.

Everything was grist to his mill and many colleagues and friends turned to his Wednesday column and found with a start that they were actually in it. Only the names were changed to protect the guilty!

He also used his keen eye for detail to paint pictures of places so deftly that the reader was able to share his feelings for that time and place as if they had actually been there.

16 August, 1989

Adolf - and his part in my father's downfall

WHEN first I met my father I was nearly seven and he was on crutches. He had carelessly allowed an anti-aircraft gun to crush his right foot. He painted a vivid picture of blood escaping from his boot like black bubbles.

When last we met he was naked, cancerous and incontinent. He died an ignominious death. Following a lifetime's pattern of mutual animosity, we exchanged few words. It wasn't all his fault.

Musing over the upcoming 50th anniversary of the outbreak of war, I came across the only thing he had left in the world - his Army service and pay book. That was my inheritance, courtesy of the binding values of Sellotape.

Within its brown covers was the story of how he became a displaced person, wild, permanently unsettled and pursued by a moody cloud of Stygian intensity. Hitler inexorably altered his life.

By proxy, he also changed mine. The man who came home was a stranger and an intruder. He was an unpredictable animal fired by an insatiable urgency to compensate for all those lost years.

Practically until the day he died the war dominated his mind. Any lull in a conversation would open the gates to memories which inevitably began with, "I remember when I was in the Army . . . "

Like most youngsters I automatically switched off, bored by reminiscences which for me were firmly a part of history. Only in later life did I grasp the implications of his prosaic meanderings.

He was an intelligent and artistic man, but basically simple. Had Adolf not interfered, he would have aspired to nothing greater than being an old-fashioned grocer who took pride in being able to bone a ham properly.

But he had not the *nous* to capitalise on his talents as an artist, a natural pianist and a skilled carpenter. Instead, he chose to assiduously train for a place in the Welsh national drinking team.

He was plucked from the heartland of North Wales, garbed in khaki and sent to foreign parts. He earned a couple of medals, three stripes and, according to that tattered pay book, his conduct was exemplary.

A model soldier laying his life on the line for buttons in North Africa and Italy. It was a massive change of lifestyle for someone who never went farther than Conwy for his holidays.

The Welsh peasant had become somewhat cosmopolitan and had flirted daily with death. Men died at his side. Civvy street could never supply the same surge of adrenalin. It was the biggest event of his humdrum life.

Once home, he threw himself into training with unstinted dedication. He had the capacity, but not the temperament. We feared his footsteps on the path, wondering who would be first through the door - Dr Jekyll or Mr Hyde.

Worse, he was wedded to a tough widow whose tongue was customised by Gillette, had A-levels in sarcasm and was a practised *agent provocateur.* It was a volatile marriage of TNT and gelignite, simultaneously entertaining and distressing.

They were the ultimate paradox. They could not live together and they could not live apart. I was very young when I decided to cut them out of my will. They were intolerable.

It took me years to realise that the old man, who remained a querulous stranger until his death, was marked for life by that bloody interlude in the desert. He stepped from behind a grocer's counter into a theatre of petrifying war.

It was a gigantic stride for a young man to whom being sent to Brecon to enlist was an adventure. On the platform of Wrexham railway station an acquaintance asked, "Did you volunteer, Trevor?"

"No," he replied. "But I'd be the first bugger to volunteer to get out." From that we can easily deduce that he was not the most enthusiastic of conscripts. And who could blame him?

It's what the war did to him that's important. There has never been compensation for stolen years or the distortion of personality. He might have been a good husband and father given the chance.

Instead, he dwelt in a desert of antiquated memories and life was never more roseate than when viewed through the bottom of a glass. Then it would start. "When I was in the Army . . . "

Minds and eyes would glaze over. The war was a long time ago. It took ages and lots of thinking to realise what it meant to him. A significant chunk of his being was purloined and potential death was a permanent shadow on his shoulder.

So it was for lots of other men. They returned far more equable and stable than Trevor. But war can damage your health. To emerge from it alive is a victory in itself.

I didn't like him and could not weep at his funeral. But after looking at that frayed and tatty pay book with its impersonal information, I think I now understand him.

5 March, 1987

Oh, to be in bandit country

LAST WEEK I got slightly tight with a knight. It would have been much like getting tiddly with anyone else except that he was Irish, an absolute hoot and kept kissing my wife's hand. What, I wondered was so repellent about my hand?

Sir John ("Call me Jack") Swinson is the kind of knight you want to hug (which I did) and take home to put on the mantelpiece (which I didn't). One of his aides was moved to refer to him as the shortest knight of the year. He deserves better.

He may be small, but I am here to tell you that Jack is a big man. You have to be some kind of giant to traverse this country and, more-or-less straight-faced tell people that Northern Ireland is a great location for a vacation.

I've been to Ulster twice and he is undeniably right. There are parts of it which are optically orgiastic and there are others which God specifically designed to deprive you of oxygen. Breathtaking.

However, Jack has to cope with minor criticisms of the province. There are those churlish enough to mention such sinister initials as IRA, INLA, UDA and then have the effrontery to query the free-flowing liberalism of that close friend of The Vatican, Ian Paisley.

Jack's great merit is that his eyes twinkle like a Bonfire Night sky. When he looks at you directly and says that these organisations are tearing themselves apart and are all but finished, you feel decidedly out-twinkled.

And what meaningful questions can you put to a man who begins his publicity hype by recounting the tale of how Belfast was hit by a typhoon which caused £40 million worth of improvement? The rest of his speech was ruined by my raucous laughter.

Jack didn't mind a bit. In fact, he promised that before he was through he would crack my ribs. Not physically, you understand but with more of the humour which makes the resilient people of Northern Ireland so special.

He is chairman of its tourist board, a job which one imagines is only marginally less difficult than selling extended weekends in Ethiopia. He was obviously chosen for this post for his patent ability to flog snow to Eskimos.

But, I ventured to suggest did he not have the toughest task in Britain? "Have another couple of oysters while I order you some more whiskey," said the little smoothie. It was all I could do to stop myself booking a week in Bandit Country.

It turns out that these days his job is a lot easier. A successful marketing operation in America (where else?) has brought over droves of Yanks whose roots are buried deep in the province.

Some shrewdly invested money brought over travel writers who were fêted, supplied with cars and allowed to roam Ulster at will. They went home and wrote nice things with only the occasional reference to the sight of a soldier toting a rifle.

The accumulative result was that last year Northern Ireland had 800,000 visitors. It wasn't exactly jackpot time, but for a place smaller than Yorkshire it was like empty veins getting eight pints of protein-enriched plasma.

It did a power of good for those living in rural areas whose existence depends on selling lavish Irish hospitality and glasses of a notoriously strong stout which, if in good condition, can take up to 10 minutes to serve. It's always a good idea to have a drink while you're waiting.

Sir John convinced me that Noraid is finished, as are all the other goons who cannot see further than the end of a gun barrel. Now that the mellowness of that memorable night has been dispelled, I still desperately hope that he is right.

His part of the world has inherited fragments of Paradise, spots so beautiful they could stop the heart of an ox if it had an ounce of sensibility between its horns. The goons have done a great disservice to a good bit of earth.

Someone in the group ventured the opinion that Ulster has too many Roman Catholics, too many Protestants and not enough Christians. I agreed. There is a surfeit of people gorging themselves on religion while starving themselves of Christianity.

Anyway, I did not feel the least bit guilty about getting a bit squiffy. My night with John was a blessed release from a week of trauma looking after two children supercharged with hooliganistic energy and filial rivalry.

Along with doing the cooking and being up to the elbows in Fairy Liquid, I was also the weary and short-tempered arbiter of many a dispute involving sneaky clouts and rending cries.

There was only momentary consolation when the youngest flung herself in my lap and lisped, "I love you, Daddy." It took several minutes to blink away the tears. There was no emotion involved, just the pain of her right knee in my squelchy bits.

With more than a twinge of conscience I cheated like mad on my paternal duties. As soon as the going got tough and my disciplinary bellows lost their steam, I flicked on the television. Thank goodness for the children's channel on cable TV.

On the one day when it wasn't freezing or pouring down we went to the park and endlessly played on the slide a peculiar family game known as, "I'll bite your bum." I missed every time but scored an awful lot of points on the laughter scale.

We bought ice-creams with which the eldest decorated her coat and the youngest used to turn herself into a reverse image of Al Jolson. By this time I was doing a grand impression of someone in need of specialist care.

It came as a great relief to get out of the house, swig some whiskey and wallow in the company of Sir John - the Knight who made my day.

5 November, 1987

Conwy: All I have to do is dream

IT WAS on a sun-warmed apron of grass beneath the early pre-Barratt structure of Conwy Castle that I first met Holden Caulfield.

Acned and insecure, he was threshing about in puberty's turbulent waters, every bit as treacherous as the currents swirling beneath the suspension bridge.

In today's climate Holden would be dismissed as a wimp badly in need of a re-wiring job. In fact, he was the touching and sadly funny hero of J.D. Salinger's masterly study of adolescence, *The Catcher in The Rye.*

I devoured it in one sitting and decided that Conwy, with some help from Salinger, had just given birth to my future. I would be a writer over whose books young people would pore entranced while reclining on verdant slopes to the back-ground music of rippling streams.

Well, we all go through our daft phases and my dreamy aspirations were reduced to striving to be a labourer worthy of his hire. But whenever the *hiraeth* fixes its pincers on my sleeve and tugs me unprotesting back to Wales, it is always to that tumbling, river-lapped, walled town that I like to return.

Seen from the bridge it is almost absurdly picturesque, like an over-romanticised three-dimensional canvas by a commercial artist who gulped a fistful of potent stimulants before applying sable bristles to palette. That first sighting always interferes with my respiration.

Within its arched, history-reeking perimeter sits a high stack of personal memories ranging from ankle-socked boyhood holidays through to Rabelaisian occasions when my candle was aflame at both extremities.

Conwy is my Llaregub. When winter strips her of tourists like leaves from the bough, she reverts to that gossipy hen-coop of which is essentially a village. There are those who say you couldn't plant a Russian spy there without his cover being blown inside a day. Not even if he spoke fluent Welsh.

The local intelligence network eclipses that of MI5. Incredibly sensitive noses can unearth the seeds of juicy tittle-tattle in the same way that French hogs dig up the succulent truffle. "It's much worse than the average small town," I was told.

"Questions about one's business are embarrassingly direct and you have to use quite sharp words to fend off malicious gossip." It seems the truth is not always essential to a tale that will have the citizenry delightedly squawking like gulls welcoming the arrival of a fully-laden fishing smack.

This time of year street life virtually dies at 4 pm. Some businesses close down for winter and some forever. Many budding entrepreneurs have made the costly discovery that Conwy is only a goldmine for a few fleeting weeks. Once there is room for the natives to bestride their own pavements again, so expands the space in traders' wallets.

At least one void has been filled, though. Work on the town's own version of the chunnel has brought an influx of abled-bodied men, especially the handsome Dutch, to breathe new life into the interminably long, dark nights of the local maidens and Polly Garters.

Not that they can any longer cement international relations in the back row of The Palace. It ceased to be a cinema two years ago and who but the most unromantic could bill and coo to raucous cries of, "Two little ducks, all the twos"? Who could click in competition with "clickety-click"?

In my youth The Palace helped to while away many an evening, its grand facade always fronted by an amiable dwarf who, in his much adorned commissionaire's uniform, looked like the successful leader of a bloodless *coup d'etat* in Lilliput. He is long gone, as is Peter.

Peter was the outrageously bluff landlord of The Liverpool Arms, the quayside magnet for posing weekend sailers trying to rub shoulders with men who earn their living from the estuary. Peter did his gushing Flying Officer act with them all, only ever reserving his cool treatment for hippies and leather-clad bikers.

Many of these species never heard his *sotto voce* reference to their membership of "The Great Unwashed". He was always polite and outgoing and, despite a hint of snobbery, a colourful part of the quay.

As is Margaret Williams, owner of the smallest house in Britain, who is known for her ability to maintain a tolerant smile while answering a torrent of asinine questions from the thousands of visitors who poke their heads through this curiosity's door.

You can cross the living quarters in two short strides. Put your foot on the bottom stair and your head is already in the bedroom. Multi-lingual tapes endlessly trip out the dwelling's history (it is thought to be 16th century) yet she is still asked if she lives there.

Were it to be occupied by Peter Rabbit it would be deemed overcrowded. It's been in Maggie's family since her great grandfather rescued it from threatened demolition in 1900 and turned it into a now famous attraction. It passed to her mother who died this year, aged 88.

She and her five helpers are among a handful of townsfolk who still cling to the habit of donning national dress for the season. Others have let it slide, much to the disappointment of visitors who seek to inhale every ounce of atmosphere the place can yield.

At the end of the jetty lies the now silent Queen Victoria, a "back in time for tea" water-bus owned by Bryn, son of Rowland "Rollie" Hughes, whose family have reaped the river as mussel fishermen and pleasure trip operators for 400 years.

They are as much a part of Conwy as the jackdaws which cackle and caw on the upper reaches of Edward I's castle. The birds give their name to a local society, membership of which is limited to those born within the town's walls. The advent of maternity homes meant there are comparatively few.

Most are in their 40s, but they can boast a two-year-old so anxious to share this exclusivity that he decided to be born in a doctor's surgery. He will grow up to enjoy the jackdaws' social life which defrosts the nights of this dank, dark quarter of the year.

Throughout the community it is a time for renewing friendships temporarily split asunder by tourism. If Conwy offers little in the way of big-town diversions, there is usually a party or get-together at which the people can become themselves again, the demands and impositions of the sightseers out of sight and mind.

Hibernation is not total, but there's an unfamiliar hush in the streets and the merest ripple of activity on the quay where the cheery Keith the Fish is still peddling empty-eyed creatures destined to fill large frying-pans or baking trays.

We used to buy our fish from a shop with a great open slab behind which worked a sloe-eyed beauty who took my nervous hand on many a stroll down the Marine Walk. At the end was a gate which led to the hillocked woodland where we kissed and I tried to close my mind and nostrils to the lingering aroma of her occupation.

The shop now houses a building society, just a few doors up from the

Blue Bell pub where Griff, the late landlord, once presented me with a whole salmon. This was to recognise my status as the son of the man with whom he enthusiastically bent elbows once a year.

It is said that you should never go back to a place of happy memories, because changes make for disappointment. Very little alters in Conwy from which Edward, cocking a regal snook at the Commission for Racial Equality, banned the Welsh. What a comeback we made.

Here and there you might find a trendy new bistro or an ethnic fashion boutique next to an earthy traditional craft shop. But it is the sheer beauty and durability of Conwy's stones and timbers which focus the camera of one's mind.

Even the police station resembles a listed building, and might be one for all I know. I never tire of the Elizabethan magnificence of Plas Mawr nor cease to marvel at Aberconwy House, built in 1300 and the oldest in town. We shall not see the day when it is bombed into oblivion like the anti-social high-rise flats which have blighted our century.

Conwy's constancy has kept my memories intact and I have only two minor regrets. One is that I never created my own Caulfield. The other is that a potentially beautiful relationship was marred by the scent of the fishmonger's slab.

26 November, 1986

Slipping back with Freud

IT MIGHT have been a genuine sense of nostalgia, or maybe it was an act of romantic theatricality, but when my father died recently I felt a need to take a last look at our old house. Quality brick, but as ugly as ever.

I never did like the place, but it remains a charmless repository of so many memories, good and bad, but mostly bad. Freud should have been lying on our sofa when Hitler was trying to straighten out kinky lines on the globe and what he perceived as ethnic aberrations.

I left the car's engine running because it was meant to be but a brief visit. Then I caught sight of Dicky's house. Dicky ruled the street because he wore a fez - courtesy of a sea-going brother - and owned Speedy Gonzales.

Speedy was a hedonistic white mouse who eschewed stud fees because he so loved his job. Show him a doe and he made an instant withdrawal from his sperm bank. So prodigious were his matings that, at one time, the street was in danger of having to call in a specialist musician from Hamelin.

Dicky was also leader of The Black Hand gang, whose membership was swollen to two when I became a lieutenant. We tied lengths of cotton to door knockers so that we could irritate from a safe distance, pushed childish notes through letter-boxes and took turns to wear the fez. We were a dangerous mob.

Across the street was the home of a woman who was forever to be known as Dirty Lucy. This soubriquet had nothing to do with personal hygiene, but everything to do with the American servicemen for whom she showed a marked preference. She was never forgiven for spurning the local swains.

"The Yanks know how to treat a woman," she was often quoted as saying. One of them treated her to a baby but neglected to leave a forwarding address when he returned Stateside. The news was greeted with almost celebratory malice and poor Lucy was branded forever.

A couple of doors away lived Eric, the resident bad boy who beat up his wife and children quite regularly and boasted about having been in prison. "I've done seven years or more," he would bellow into the still night, drunk as a skunk as he staggered home from the pub. Eric was never invited to coffee mornings and was never seen at church socials.

His next-door neighbours had a daughter called Jessie who was always "up the fields with the big lads." Dicky and I had to wait several years before we knew the significance of her fondness for the rural perimeters of our suburb. That's where we were later to do our courting. It hardly ever seemed to rain in those days.

If it did, then you could always climb the school gate, sneak past Billy's caretaker lodge and find shelter in the coke shed. Not warm, but dry, and a spirited session of necking was guaranteed to warm the early frosts.

My eye settled on the house where Peter had lived. He was a braggart who commanded a certain awe among the kids because he had actually lived in America - in New York for goodness sake! He would strut into the chip shop and loudly call for "Ten cents' worth of fries."

Peter wanted everyone to know that he had dwelled in the Big Apple. He didn't want anyone to know when he was involved in a homosexual scandal, so he lay on his bed, turned on the gas and went permanently to sleep. The street seethed with so much gossip that Lucy wasn't back-stabbed for weeks.

The local bobby, a scamp in uniform, had never been so busy. The tragic event interfered with his drinking. For years people talked of the day he was quaffing a pint when his sergeant walked into the pub. The glass disappeared under his cape and remained there during the long walk back to the station, where it was hidden in a toilet until Sarge cleared off.

Mrs Kelly's shop is still on the corner, although the proprietor is long gone. That's where we bought our sweets with ration coupons and hoped to catch a glimpse of Mrs K's daughter, Cynthia. I fancied her like mad, simply because Dicky told me to.

I still thought girls were soppy and found his explanation of how babies were made quite incredible. So did my mother when I told her. She clipped my ear and told me to stay away from him, but the street wasn't long enough to avoid the boy who knew too much for his age.

It stopped at a low mesh fence which marked the beginning of what we knew as Parker's Field, which separated our humble homes from the posh private houses a mile away. It was almost as effective as the Berlin Wall, as well as being a social divide, because Mr Parker chased trespassers with a fury which made us fleet of foot at a tender age. Now you can drive through it.

The pasture has gone to make way for one of those twee little housing estates whose gardens host conventions of little gnomes with fishing-poles and horticultural implements. Gone, too, is the marsh where the entrepreneurial Dicky and I gathered ladysmock to sell at threepence a bunch.

We never made any money from that venture, nor from scouring Fatty Thomas's field (at the other end of the street) for cowpats which we took home in buckets to sell to our respective fathers as manure.

Around the corner is the church where I once sang in the choir before being slung out for misbehaving during the Wednesday evening practice. Once a year we were given three shillings and taken to Southport for the day. We felt we were crossing a continent to somewhere called Abroad.

It is said that you should never go back to any place of which you have fond memories - unless you want your memories shattered. Mine are still intact despite all the changes.

I must have sat outside the old house for ten minutes. Then I revved up and drove off, taking with me all those hours of gladness which, like our youth, are too soon gone.

9 October, 1990

Still so much for this Katie to do

FOR SOMEONE who has been poor, been on the dangerous end of Fascist guns, committed to a "loony bin" by a cruel, amoral father, and known many desperate dark hours, Katie Boyle still exudes a voracious appetite for life.

Titled by both birth and marriage she is very much a working woman, both as an earner and a volunteer. Watching her in action you cannot escape the impression of perpetual motion, nor the rather forlorn wish that half her energy could be yours.

Yet, this overtly personable woman is 64. Was it not time, I facetiously suggested, that she spent her days picking dahlias, cutting off dead rose heads and tending to her lovely garden?

"Good heavens, no," she declaimed. "Maybe in ten or 15 years time, but I could never retire. I shall always be busy and there is so much to come. Even death will be an adventure because I believe in a certain continuity.

"I'd like a death-bed scene, but I would want it to be quick. We Roman Catholics always want it to be quick, but I'm a bad Catholic because I'm still married to my first husband, who gave me an excellent reference before I married Peter (impresario Sir Peter Saunders) and we are still good friends."

Sir Peter is her third husband, the first being the Earl of Shannon followed by Greville Baylis, Lloyds underwriter, former diplomat and city blade, who obtained a far from amicable divorce to marry her.

It was a spirited union marred by the discovery that Greville had had a three-year affair with another woman. Katie went on to become involved with a married man, generating that beloved brand of gossip which mixes self-righteousness with moral indignation.

Katie survived it and was reconciled with Greville who, as he lay dying in 1976, talked of the "fantastic 20-year innings" they had had and of the wonderful marriage it had been. She assuaged her grief by engaging in an exhausting work schedule.

Cautiously, I inquired if her track record implied a great liking of men and a preference for their company. "I have strong female friendships and I have never been promiscuous," she said firmly.

"I have never been a happy mistress and am definitely the marrying kind, which could be why men seem more than happy to marry me. I'm not the kind who lights up the moment a man enters the room and women don't seem frightened of me."

We were speaking as she made the final preparations for the Katie Boyle show in which she has replaced her good buddy Judith Chalmers. It involves her getting up at 5.45 am each day and being at the BBC in time to edit listeners' letters before going on air at 9.30 am.

"Anyone who thinks doing a request show is easy is deluding themselves," she said. "I'm not allowed to discuss the day's newspapers nor to do interviews, so I have thought of something totally different which has yet to be agreed."

Gloria Hunniford told her to make it her own show by stamping her personality on it. She intended to emulate the brevity of her broadcasting idol, Ken Bruce and hoped that would be understood by the listener who had complained of her patronising attitude.

"Brisk, yes, but never patronising," she said. The stand-in period was brief - did she hanker doing it for longer? I can't go on forever getting up at that time of day, and besides, I want to concentrate more on Peter and give him time. I dread : 'If onlys'."

That could also mean her giving up work in Europe, where her name is still inextricably linked with the Eurovision Song Contest and her faultless multi-linguism. "I used to stand up there looking clever and flamboyant but, actually, I was right at home with languages I learned as a child," she said.

Katie has also done much other work over the channel, some of it winning for her the Radio and Television Personality of Europe Award. But it was an award made early this month which tickled her pink.

The readers of a magazine voted her one of the three most stylish women in Britain which, "at my vintage," absolutely delighted her. "I see no point in being blasé about these things. If you are blasé, it's an insult to the people who voted for you," she said.

Although Katie protests that her wardrobe is a hotchpotch, she cannot deny that innate sense of style which seems to go hand-in-hand with having been born an Italian. She loves colour and scent, although it must have no connection with animal experiments.

Animals are her passion and these days she is often to be found on dawn patrol for Battersea Dogs Home, collecting sad strays from police stations. "I've never been bitten yet, which just shows what kindness can do," Katie said.

"You have to remember in dealing with a dog you are in reality dealing with a wolf. You must establish a relationship from the start, letting them know who's boss and at the same time showing them kindness."

"I can tell you're not a dog person, but don't you think these four are well-behaved?" she asked, indicating her 'liquorice allsorts' slumbering on her armchair. All had been cruelly treated before falling into her lap and on their feet.

"I would love to have a TV show promoting centres where owners could be taught about the business of rehabilitation and one on which we could fight those awful puppy farms. The law does not back up the RSPCA in these matters."

Did she not feel she could do more good by channelling these energies into similar causes for children? "I do a lot with children but there are people more knowledgeable and experienced than I. I can't divide myself up into any more pieces."

There are so many instances of cruelty but I simply cannot take them all on. If I can save a few of the victims then I feel I will be doing something useful," she said.

She produced some old photographs of the asylum to which her father, a Russian-Italian nobleman, had her committed. Theirs had always been a stormy relationship since he divorced her half-English mother and Katie was expelled from four of the six schools to which she was sent.

Not that she was a maverick, but they were strict and she did not see why rules could not be ever so slightly bent. During the war she discovered her father was courting the Germans, Mussolini's Fascists and hiding partisan weapons in the family chapel.

This knowledge became dangerous when, after her stepmother's death, her father became a moody tyrant who held her prisoner in her own bedroom for three months. Katie made a dramatic escape and joined her lover who, after three days, was taken away by the partisans.

After being shot at and witnessing horrible acts of war on the streets, Katie found herself back home. With the Allies advancing daily, her father probably felt that she could seriously compromise him.

His harsh and vengeful solution was to have her committed, a nightmarish ordeal which ended only when her mother was located in Switzerland and returned to Italy to help in her rescue.

Later came a new life in England, work as a model and then as a television hostess at a time when game shows proliferated. She became a personality whose star has only occasionally dimmed.

There are memories and relatives enough to keep alive those terrible war years in Italy and experiences which might have repressed a lesser person.

Not our Katie. Like a gourmet she looks upon life as a feast and has clearly yet to eat her fill.

13 November, 1986

Tracking down the unreal Bulman

AS A SPECTATOR sport, the making of a TV show ranks only slightly above reading an anthology of vinyl floor coverings, or a dissertation on whether sex will ever yield to the ascendancy of the bicycle. It is mind-bogglingly boring.

It is even less gripping if you dined too well the previous night and little green men seem intent on building a new stretch of motorway through your head. That's how it was in draughty Didsbury on Monday morning as I watched Don Henderson slamming down the bonnet of a car which looked in danger of imminent disintegration.

When he did it for the eighth time I took my acute sense of *déjà vu* to a cafe to feed black coffee to my noisy road-gang. Don later arrived with the plastic carrier bag which has become a trademark on the set of Bulman. Off the set, it doubles as his briefcase. No-one could accuse him of looking like the man from the Pru.

While he spurns the star image, Granada TV give him the treatment. I found myself in the rear of a chauffeur-driven white limousine in which you could have played a game of pool if someone had brought along a table. It whisks him from location to location and it took us to an upmaket pub for lunch.

That famous voice is a wondrous mixture - two of gravel to one generous lading of sand - and he's lucky to have it. Some years ago he discovered by accident that he had throat cancer. There was no pain to warn him that he was on the road to losing the power of speech.

A course of treatment did the trick, leaving him with vocal sounds which he likens to being uttered by a frog with a bucket over its head. Don gave up smoking for years, but now, when he's working, chain-smokes aromatic French cigarettes and recognises how silly it is.

We chain-smoked together as I asked him about persistent rumours that he is eccentric. "Not at all," he said, "but people who are don't know it. I don't suppose for one minute that Hitler regarded himself as evil and was probably convinced he was merely doing great things for his country."

A bit of an eccentric comparison, I thought, particularly as he was unaware that it was his birthday. Co-star Siobhan Redmond assured him it was, having already planned a surprise champagne party for him on the set of what passes for Bulman's flat.

Pressed about his age, Don took a stab at 54. A quick sum on a beer mat revealed that he was 55 and, yes, it was his birthday. He celebrated by ploughing through a monstrous mound of ice-cream which he said tasted like angel's sweat. I took this to be a quirky, if unsavoury sounding, tribute to the confection.

As delicately as possible I broached the question of the Henderson-Bulman sense of sartorial elegance. He admits to owning a suit, but said it took something akin to an Act of Parliament to get him into it. His wedding ensemble sounded a dream - jeans, open-neck shirt and a sports jacket.

He is married to actress Shirley Stelfox, who keeps popping up in Brookside, and they live with their three children in Stratford on Avon. I warmed to him immensely when he confessed that, like me, he is fairly useless about the house and tends to be a stay-at-home.

Socialising tends to muck up his work schedule and he has been known to fall asleep over the soup at a dinner party, in the cinema and, just as embarrassing, in the front row of a theatre. Normally he is in bed by 10 at the latest, learning his lines.

His memory must be passing good, although there was the time he forgot his own name. He was trying to telephone a big director and had mentally prepared himself for battle with a battery of secretaries. However, he got straight through to the great man and was immediately flustered.

Instead of the conventional greetings, the director barked, "What's your name?" Don panicked to the point where he was frantically searching his pockets for some identification. "He started getting angry and I giggled because I was being so stupid. I looked in a hand mirror, but I couldn't put a name to the face and then I got frightened," Don said.

Needless to say, he failed to get the part he was after.

He loves to tell the story of the day he and three other actors, all dressed as tramps, were being driven to a location in the big limo. It stopped at traffic lights alongside the car of an obvious Colonel Blimp type.

Its occupant was clearly stunned to see these scruffs travelling in luxury and became visibly agitated. Don wound down the window and said, "We're all going to Blackpool for the day and it's costing us nothing. Paid for out of the rates. Great innit?"

Blimp went puce and Don still chuckles at the thought of his writing an angry letter to The Times about the disgraceful excesses of the welfare state.

The same cheeky sense of humour made him a professional actor at the ripe old age of 38 when, juiced up after a session at the pub, he accepted a dare to go for an audition with the RSC. He was so successful that his earnings plummeted by £88 to £12 a week.

From well-off salesman to rookie actor in one flabbergasting swoop. Six years working with such giants as Paul Schofield, then ten in television and films. Along the way he made George Bulman part of the public consciousness.

He does not exude the insecurities which beset other members of his profession, but claims that they are there all the same. "This job is like having a licence to practise schizophrenia," he said. It's pretending to be someone else."

I watched him climb into the limo, this professional scruff with the plastic bag. Was I saying goodbye to Henderson or Bulman? Then, like my little green men, he was gone.

2 November, 1989

Where all our yesterdays are sweet as wine

AT ABOUT 2 pm yesterday, a little man with lots of forgotten yesterdays in his eyes wandered into Yates' Wine Lodge in Great Charlotte Street, Liverpool, and was greeted by a storm of applause. He had obviously been there before.

The licensee gently guided him back into the street and dropped him a few coins on condition that he did not return. The wee devil was back in a couple of minutes, demanding a bigger pay-off.

He was back on the street in a flash, mainly, I suspect because he epitomised everyone's prejudiced view of the stereotype Yates' customer - vacant, dazed and addicted to cheap wine. It was not his day.

How could he know that the company had invited the media to inspect £150,000 worth of refurbishment, including a magnificent maple floor, in order to take a distinctly jaded image very much up-market?

At that moment, his obviously well-known face didn't fit. Neither did mine, but, fortified by a couple of glasses of Aussie white, I braved it out. They call it white, but it looks and tastes more like tawny sherry. Curious.

I talked to Christopher Martin-Bird, the company's chairman, who is the fourth generation of his family to run a concern started by teetotaller Peter Yates in Oldham in 1844. He apparently coined the phrase, "A day without wine is like a day without sunshine," and his customers have basked in it ever since.

He got the idea from his visits to Portugal, and according to a lovely PR lady, was a retailer way ahead of his time when he introduced Boseley beef sandwiches.

He raised his own herd of cattle to produce the meat and bought a bakery to provide the bread. Even today, his influence still pervades our way of life. Most of the plastic bottles of wine supplied on aircraft are from Yates' stock.

Mr. Martin-Bird was a bit reluctant to talk about the image of his customers, which, seemingly, prevails only in Liverpool and Manchester. Elsewhere, the bibulous are not regarded in the same deprecating way.

The typical tippler is now aged between 25 and 35, comes from any strata of life you care to mention, and enjoys drinking on the cheap. Port and sherry used to be the favourites, but now Aussie white is the ticket to blissful oblivion.

I bumped into the very likeable Phil Young, author of the Scouseology books, who freely admitted that he had been a Yates' habitueé in the Sixties. "You met a great cross-section of society and it was entirely classless," he said.

"It was cheap and full of action, movement and drama. I heard some great comments in this bar, which is where I saw the last white £5 note in existence. It belonged to a lady of the streets and had been given to her by a Norwegian sailor.

"He was the only man she every truly loved, and he gave it to her in exchange for an entire weekend. Because she loved him, the note came to her to represent a love letter. I thought there was something beautiful about its symbolism."

Phil waxed lyrical about the ambience and recalled that anyone who drank too much and ended up in the Main Bridewell for the night was said to be "in-off the white" - a witty ambiguity not culled from the game of snooker, but relating to the 2cc Honda fuel that had been imbibed.

Phil thought Yates' public perception misconceived. "You could find yourself standing next to an intellectual, a football player, or a rogue," he said. "A lot of people were frightened to come, especially nice girls. There were lots of night-time girls and pros.

"There were also upper middle-class women ...pretentious lushes, who always had a sob story to tell. They were bores who always told the same tale, but you had to remember that they were basically unhappy and needed someone to talk to.

"You could drink in here for a couple of hours, spend virtually nothing, and be well on, by which I mean drunk. Aussie white created the glory days before you became responsible and learned to grow up."

Licensee Charlie Gorman told me about Clicker Clarke, one of his best cutomers, who died last year. There were two coaches of mourners - one for those who were barred from the Great Charlotte Street wine bar, and one for those who were not."He was a little coloured man and no-one really knew him" said Charlie. "But when he died, we had the funeral from here. We still see the same customers every day and know them so well we don't have to ask what they want to drink.

"The only trouble we get is from football fans who are total strangers, but now we have learned to keep the doors closed when a big match is on. The locals are great and donate a lot of money to charity. We had letters from Maggie Thatcher and the Queen saying they were unable to attend, so we raffled them."

To be in a Yates' wine lodge is to dwell in another world. There are so many forgotten yesterdays in so many eyes.

And it's still the only place I know where someone was actually paid not to come in....

15 June, 1988

A severe dose of Senna bods

YOU WILL, I am quite sure, have already met Mrs Senna Pod. She is immediately identifiable by the set of her lips. When acutely pursed they are capable of converting an entire season's grape yield into an instant crop of withered raisins.

Her importance is evident because she owns at least two Biros and a white overall positively rigid with starch. She also wears a look calculated to make you feel like a recent deposit from the mucky end of a mongrel.

In another life she might have been a traffic warden, gleefully slapping fixed penalties on cripples' crutches for dithering too long on busy streets. In a correctional institution, she would be the one to demand lights out immediately after Blue Peter.

It's not that she is inherently mean, merely that she suffers delusions of adequacy and probably favours directoires a shade too tight just above the knee. She has not a vestige of authority but fabricates enough to exercise it to the hilt.

Do you recognise her now? You must do. I have yet to enter a doctor's surgery without failing to immediately pick out the Pod, flourishing like a stand-up-and-fight cactus under the plate glass of her own personal Checkpoint Charlie.

It is here that the lame, sick and lazy come face to grim face with Godzilla's mother-in-law, a species for whom clerical duties give insufficient scope for officious muscle-flexing. The seductive white coat induces fantasies of being a consultant-in-waiting, rather than a helping hand in the waiting room.

This is the woman who, over the telephone, performs contortions to persuade you to prolong your ailment for three or four days until she can fit you in. If, in the meantime your leg should drop off, Senna will probably tell you to hop it.

As the self-appointed buffer between the GP and what she perceives as galloping hypochondria she will, however, yield an inch. This gets you no nearer the doctor but wins the week's special prize of Senna's famed diagnostic technique.

From anything up to five miles distant she picks up your telephonic vibes, hazards an ill-educated guess at what seems to be the trouble and promises that doctor will write a prescription. This can be picked up later in the year, any time after noon. Meanwhile, don't die of any complications that Telecom did not transmit down the line.

My current Mrs Pod is nothing if not consistent, in that she seems to be universally disliked by all whose visas she has scrutinised at Checkpoint Charlie. One GP has privately admitted they do have "communications problems" - which probably means the doctors have not been following her instructions.

Under a long-standing arrangement made at my GP's insistence, I turned up at the surgery last week and told our Senna whom I had come to see. She quickly flicked through her register of pests and nuisances and assumed the smile of a striking mamba. I swear her eyes lit up as she hissed: "You're not booked in."

Wearily, and not for the first time, I reiterated the arrangement. "It is not the doctor's job to do the booking in," she said with scarcely-concealed irritation. "I'm merely doing what I was told," I replied and stalked off to the waiting room.

Mrs Pod sensed that the unthinkable might be about to happen - a serious loss of face to something called a patient who had flouted her Holy Writ. Not only that, but the medic had contravened the rules. Her rules. It was unthinkable.

You could practically hear another grape harvest dying on the vine as she strode into the surgery. She emerged 30 seconds later and essayed a smile thin enough to shave with. "Doctor will see you in a moment," she said. To the surprise of other patients and much to my chagrin she added: "You must be very important, that's all I can say."

Cheeky bitch. If I were the least little bit important she surely would not have spoken to me in that embarrassing way. I was about to say so but she was already back behind the glass screen totting up points scored and lost. War had been declared.

It would not matter so much if Senna presided over an appointments system which actually worked, but her's doesn't. At other surgeries I have attended, one's name was called out by the resident Pod at roughly the time agreed.

At this one the patients have been allowed to impose their own first-come-first-served system. So if the dragon has given you the 10 am slot, you might still be waiting an hour later - not that it is of consequence to someone who owns two Biros.

She's a tough lady. You suspect that were she a man she'd be the type to jog home immediately after a vasectomy wearing nothing but rough calico shorts. If she has an adoring following it can only be that she has been ingratiating herself with her aged parents.

Senna is not alone in her frailty of succumbing to what I think of as the uniform syndrome. There are countless numbers who do a Jekyll and Hyde once they don a peaked cap or get a splash of scrambled egg on their epaulets.

Mrs Pod has done a disservice to all those receptionists who are mindful of the fact that no-one hangs about a surgery for fun. If I have done her an injustice I really don't mind, if only to repay patients everywhere who are cowered by starch whether it be in the face, the heart or the overall.

24 December, 1986

And may all your festive fun be as Sweet as ours

WHAT ON earth is a Wuzzle? I haven't a clue. But if you care to pop around to my place at about 6.30 am tomorrow (please God, it's not earlier) all will be revealed by a kid with sleep in her eyes and hope in her heart.

My vague understanding is that a Wuzzle is a peculiar, rotund creature of amusing visage which, even without a beard, bears more than a passing resemblance to yours truly. Compliments fly thick and fast in our house.

One thing is for sure, this creation in felt and kapok was grossly overpriced and superbly marketed on the box ... along with Barbie, Sindy, the cloying Care Bears, My Little Pony, Shera (terrific legs), He-Man (grotesquely muscular), et al.

Already fully-fledged members of the acquisitive society my girls watched the commercials with saucer-size eyes and chorused, "I want one, I want one." Their cries were so loud they couldn't hear my inner voice intoning, "Tough luck, tough luck."

Had we fulfilled all their mercenary desires, we would have needed to buy another house merely to accommodate this surrogate family of plastic and furry squatters. Considering the bank manager's present mood, I need wage earners rather than dependants.

But what the hell? Tomorrow morning I will get full value for every overdrafted penny I spent. Four eyes will shine so brightly they will temporarily obscure the prospect of those fiscal missives bleaker than January itself.

Let the council whine and whinge for its exhorbitant rates. Let the bank gnaw at my vitals. Let the gas and electricity boards threaten to bankrupt me. This week my disposable income has been invested in unfettered happiness.

It will pay high dividends, if only for a comparatively short time. Within days I expect the Wuzzle to be relegated to the back row in favour of houses fashioned from cardboard boxes filched from the supermarket. What previously contained a load of Jaffa oranges or a consignment of Fairy Liquid will become a des. res. to which the Wuzzle might be invited if he's lucky.

No matter. Tomorrow there will be moments of magic I could not buy even with an extended overdraft. They will be priceless. I've already got the Kleenex handy to fake a sneeze and excuse the moistened eyes.

When the initial excitement has died down to a dull roar and muted shrieks of delight, we will drift into the kitchen for the ritual of Christmas Day breakfast. Cereals for the children and something expensive from Epernay for the seasonally dissolute parents.

The cork will be discharged across the back garden in the fervent hope it does not fragment a neighbour's bedroom window. I always aim high, but my trajectory is suspect. Then it's glasses raised to the day, to the future and to the hope of solvency.

Tomorrow will be different because of Edna Sweet. I've never met her, but she is to be my house guest for a week. All I know of her is that she is in her 70's, eats as heartily as a sparrow and, as she told me over the phone, stammers. In a 10-minute chat as warm as toast she did not once stutter.

Edna, an old friend of my wife's family, is returning to Merseyside after 30 years. She is already awash with nostalgia and I just hope that her roseate memories are not splintered by disillusionment. She won't recognise the place.

I warmed to her voice and manifest personality. She's a stranger to me, but we're already pals. Courtesy of the outrageously expensive British Telecom, an empathy was established. Within seconds I decided that Edna was sweet.

The man in her life has died, and so has her much cherished pet dog. Until we wrote, Christmas for her meant cheerless days alone in a Hastings flat that needs something like Sellafield to heat it.

She's nervous about making the six-hour journey. It's been years since she embarked on anything more adventurous than a bus trip into town. Today, at her age, she has the intrepid spirit of a pioneer.

She's coming home to a host of memories, both pleasant and painful. The vibrant Liverpool, so alive in her mind will soon be a sad corpse. It's not the city she remembers, but she must discover that for herself.

A big part of her life will run through her mind faster than a mountain stream, the memories tumbling and bubbling over the rocks of time. She is already prepared to shed a few tears.

It's our job to make sure there are also moments of pleasure, laughter and, hopefully, hilarity. Merry Christmas, I promise you, Mrs Sweet.

29 June, 1988

Where the sun of Cyprus lights a magical menu

I WAS LIMPING through Liverpool (the result of wearing odd shoes) and successfully posing as an anonymous recorder of the inconsequential when I was grabbed by the elbow and steered into a dark room.

My assailant sported a luxuriant thicket of a moustache from whose inner reaches there appeared a formidable set of teeth. Not as showy as Esther Rantzen's, but certainly better arranged.

"What you want, young man? Metaxa, whisky or ouzo?" he asked.

It was only 10 am and I was not yet ready to face the golden eye of a fried egg or Bo Derek's navel, let alone Lucifer's two-stroke rocket fuel. He then brought into play his artfully-sinuous Corps Diplomatique technique. "When you gonna give me some bloody publicity?" he bellowed.

Employing what little Greek I know, I offered him instead a kick up the bazouki. He laughed like a demented burro and said: "You one of the nicest people I ever meet," which, if you didn't know better, would suggest he has led a very sheltered life.

Anyway, I made a vague promise and left to interview a Chinese. Beggar me, I had walked only 15 yards when I was again waylaid and offered a choice of drinks.

It's one thing persuading Satan to get behind you, but quite another to stop him shoving you in the back aided by the willing shoulders of the Antoni family.

The patriarch Andreas (Andy) puts his back into everything, although I have noticed that in middle age he seems to be drifting toward indolence. He now puts in only 16 hours a day, takes Sundays off and is in danger of becoming a real sybarite.

His is the driving energy of the survivor, of a man who never again wants to know the poverty that springs from unrelenting unemployment. It drove him from Paphos on Cyprus to these shores in 1956. He was then an inexperienced youth of 18.

Four short years later, his shoulders and his hopes broadened by hard work and saving, he opened his own business - a fish and chip shop in Liverpool's Islington district.

One of his regular customers was a young girl called Cilla White who fancied herself a bit of a singer. Like her, Andy also had ambition and went on to open his restaurant in Hardman Street.

It was 12 years ago, just when that part of the city was becoming nocturnally fashionable for what North American writer Stanley Reynolds dubbed "the trendy riff-raff."

In time everyone ended up at Antoni's, tempted by succulent chunks of afelia, a lamb fasolaki as tender as a spit-roasted budgerigar and proper chips the size of torpedoes.

The ridiculously low prices were also a magnet. To eat there now is a bit like an old boys' and girls' reunion. The same people have been going since 1974.

These days they drift into the kitchen for a chat or to exchange loud badinage with the owner. When funds are short they "borrow" a meal or a bottle of wine without embarrassment, and will likely get a glass on the house.

With the help of his wife Androula, an excellent cook, Andy largely taught himself to recreate the original dishes of Cyprus. His son Christopher read books on Spanish cooking to open the restaurant just three doors away. "Don't eat at my Dad's tonight," he said. "You come here and I'll give you a good meal."

Such filial treason, especially since Dad put up the loot to launch Christopher's independent ship of fortune. Pushiness is part of family life and their work ethic.

Discretion is also one of their trademarks. Whenever I have eaten at Andy's with a woman other than she who is the wings beneath my feet, he has never batted an eyelid.

In all the years I have known him, he has never asked one ticklish question which would have me reaching for the Celtic Book of Unlikely Stories. Since my wife knew of every appointment in advance, it didn't matter. But there are places where not only do walls have ears but rather large mouths to match.

He has an instinct about people - those who wish to be referred to as "sir" and "madam", those with whom he is quickly on first-name terms and the old customers like me who are momentarily flattered to be addressed as young man or to be cussed in the friendliest way.

Modesty is also an endearing trait.

"I cook the best Greek food in Liverpool, and Liverpool Greek restaurants are giving better value for money than any in England," he said. "We have to because people here do not spend their money unwisely.

"In other cities they can afford to go out more often, but here they go out maybe once a week and make an occasion of it. Since we are away from the big estates, that is another reason why we have to be good to attract people to Hardman Street.

"We all had a bad time in the early 1980s and business went down. So we had to keep our prices low. It's a hard life with long hours, but I get all my fun socialising with the customers at their tables. Some have been coming here since they were in college."

When you walk through that door, all your senses are assailed by little bits of Greek Cyprus. It might be a trifle humble, but I know of nowhere else where you can swap insults with the boss and still share his food.

13 May, 1987

Where there's muck, there's methane and monks

ONE MORNING last week my nostrils were assailed by a strong aroma whose source was cooking under the rays of an uncommonly hot sun. I stopped momentarily to have a quick retch and to reflect on the pungent power of simmering chicken droppings.

While bent almost double to aid my coughing and heaving, I noticed that a generous coating of the odorous substance had attached itself to my new shoes. I've never been so deliriously happy.

I was in pursuit of a Cistercian monk whose pastoral skills and ingenuity had won him an anti-pollution award for converting slurry into methane gas. Not only was I treading in crap, I was also expected to write about it.

This is not to demean the achievement of Father Jim Conlon, farm manager at Bethlehem Abbey, Portglenone, Co. Antrim. It's just that I have a delicate stomach and a pronounced aversion to excreted matter.

I was on a brief odyssey in Ulster and it was thought a good idea for me to discover the properties of muck which have made the monastery almost self-suffficient in energy. Besides which, the experience might have prepared me for an O-level in muck-raking.

An appointment was made and I duly turned up at the abbey to be greeted by an aged monk with a flowing white beard. It immediately became clear that he and the outside world are barely on nodding terms.

I explained my mission and said I was from Liverpool which, not unreasonably, he seemed to equate with a distant planet. "Take a seat," he said. Before half an inch of my ample bottom made contact with the leatherette he said, "Now come with me." How very Irish.

I tried to hide a bewildered smile and followed him to a cubicle which housed a dumb waiter and one of those smart push-button telephones. "I'll ring Father Jim at the farm and let him know you're here," he told me.

He punched out the number - then lifted the receiver. "That's funny, the phone must be dead," he said. I knew instinctively there was no point in trying to explain what he was doing wrong. Delightfully dotty people find it difficult to be anything other than delightfully dotty.

The super slurry distiller failed to show, so Methusaleh gave me vague directions to the farm. "Just ask anyone for Father Jim," he said. I walked for what seemed like half a day, following my nose towards an odorous smell that doesn't quite go with the image of soft-boiled eggs.

There was not a rustic monk in sight and the noises emanating from the poultry shed suggested they were inhabited only by fowls clucking about their bowel movements. So I took to the fields.

The smell was much better, but my quest still in vain. On my way out I was stopped by a lorry driver who asked if I was in charge of the chicken houses. In any other part of the world the question would have been wounding, but this was Ireland.

O.K., my shoes had acquired a layer of chicken manure, but what about the expensive suit and flamboyant striped tie? Did I really look like a monk supervising egg collections? Given the heat, the pong and my failure, I could easily have been irritated. I opted for the Irish solution and laughed my head off.

Our schedule dictated that I had to pass up my world scoop on slurry processing (what a shame) and head for the Antrim coast. Someone should have warned us that we would need oxygen cylinders. Our collective breath was often snatched away by scenes of unimaginable beauty.

I mean, have you ever seen the Giant's Causeway? It was built centures ago by that supreme artist Mother Nature when she was going through her hexagonal period: long before Picasso dabbled with cubism. Pablo was innovative but old Ma wrote the original book on primitive art.

When you see those 38,000 symmetrical columns of basalt descending into the sea and fending off the charges of ungelded white horses, you only hope that your eyes and brain don't pop out simultaneously. To think it once stretched all the way to Scoland is too big a boggle for the mind to cope with.

The canny Irish, of course, invented a legend to justify this remarkable volcanic accident. It was constructed, they say, so that a belligerent colossus called Finn McCool could bestride it to duff up an equally oversized gent in Hibernia. Totally believable.

The causeway is now in the care of The National Trust, which has built a visitors' centre atop the steep and winding path which leads to this magnificent quirk of nature. My hour-long stay there would have been wholly pleasant had not some politically aware Irishman quizzed me about Derek Hatton. That little imp gets everywhere.

The thing about Ireland - north and south - is that people are all too ready to talk to you at the drop of a hat. If you have any reserve, prepare to cast it out. What you might regard as nosiness, they consider to be friendly "crack" - the term for having a good and interesting natter.

On we forged down a coastline which never failed to jolt one's senses. Here a vast tract of unpolluted, deserted sand, there the dramatic ruins of some ancient castle, and everywhere lovely bays alive with the sound of rolling, crested waves crashing against craggy rocks and cliffs.

My wife expected everywhere to be awash with soldiers and the RUC, but we saw only one uniformed figure. He was about 65 and patiently awaiting the tolling of the school bell so that he could safely usher the children across the road. I did not feel the least intimidated.

It is the tragedy of Ulster that the world sees only the madcap violence in pockets of Belfast and Londonderry. Beyond those mean streets is a world of rolling hills bedecked in the ochre finery of wild gorse and seascapes which might have been deposited there by some Old Master.

My only complaint was that the drinks were a mite dear. If I return, as I surely shall, I shall either have to go on the wagon or save up. The latter course seems somehow to have more appeal.

8 October, 1986

Echoes from a far parade ground, vaguely

MY RESPONSE to the first military command ever barked at me was to wonder how the corporal had so quickly assessed my mental abilities. We had known each other only five minutes when he bawled: " 'Ere, you bird-brain, come 'ere."

I committed the grave sin of smiling. In a trice our faces were a mere two inches apart, his contorted with rage. "Lissen lad, if you don't wake up I shall put you in the compound and flog you to death with a stocking full of red 'ot shit," he screamed. "And keep those eyes up or I'll poke 'em out and play marbles with 'em."

Threatened with blindness and assault with an unorthodox instrument, I tried reassuring myself that this was just part of the Army's overall plan to make a man of me. It didn't work and I had to fight back an atavistic urge to cry out, "Mum, help me." This, it seems, was a common reaction enabling NCOs to sneer, "I know your mother wouldn't like it, but your mother's not getting it."

This was my introduction to National Service and, excluding the previous 10 traumatic minutes, there were still two years to go. Already that corporal had weighted my heart with the ballast of despair and an element of fear.

I disinter this piece of personal history for two reasons. The first is that a Gallup Poll last month revealed two out of three Britons support the return of compulsory National Service for all 18-year-olds. Sadists all.

The second is the publication of a book, The Best Years of Their Lives in which former squaddies in bondage recall their experiences. The title is testimony to the memory's highly selective trick of recalling only the good times.

They could have only been the best years of anyone's lives if they had previously been shoved up chimneys or stood in for pit ponies on their days off. There must have been sick orphans who had better times.

There was a minimum of fun to be wrung from sheer misery, humiliation, degradation, living quarters as forbidding as Walton Jail and the £1 a week we were free to fritter on such goodies as blanco, Brasso, boot polish and soft yellow dusters.

The rookies resented having their careers interrupted at a time when everyone could expect to walk into a job. Career soldiers resented acting as instructors to military misfits who left as soon as they had been usefully trained.

I recall the frustration of a drill instructor faced with the physical incompetence of a huge jolly farmhand from Dorset. Clear across the parade ground he shrieked, "Why don't you lob your penis out? You march like an 'orse, you might as well look like one."

Like the rest of us the lad was convulsed, but the incident served as a metaphor for the grossly unhappy relationship between the professionals and reluctant conscripts in transit. We were the best of enemies.

We were also a source of cheap labour. Cleaning out the grease traps in the cook house stretched the mind, as did scooping the yokes from hard boiled eggs to make hors-d'oeuvres for the officers' mess. Picking up litter and raking gravel on the parade ground were also instructional.

And beware the NCO who put his head around the billet door to enquire, "Anyone here interested in music?" Those who had forgotten the wise warning never to volunteer for anything were immediately enlisted to move a piano to the sergeants' mess.

I recall with genuine pleasure the day our offensively ignorant RSM adjudged me to be deformed. My back pack would not sit correctly on my shoulders so I was assigned to emptying officers' bins rather than embarrass him during an inspection by War Office top brass.

Life in Aldershot was so awful, and such were the terrors of a General Inspection, that my comrades practically begged me for lessons in how to round their shoulders. Never before, and never since has humping garbage generated so much happiness.

Life in Nairobi was infinitely sweeter. Travel to exotic climes was the big bonus of enslavement. The CO expressed the hope that I had lots of hobbies. "The Europeans will have nothing to do with you and the black girls are likely to give you something anti-social," he smiled.

But there was a minimum of bull, an office job keeping tabs on the exiled Jomo Kenyatta, leave in Mombasa and visits to the Game Reserve. We ignored the English plumbers who had now become sanitary inspectors and referred to us as "those types".

We basked in the sun, became suicidal during the long rains, got drunk in the NAAFI and lay on our bunks dreaming of home and the glory of the four seasons. There were times when we longed for frost and snow.

We had changed but we weren't "men", we were gravel rakers and office boys who knew how to iron a uniform and shine a pair of boots. What we had in common was a burning desire to return to real life.

1 March, 1983

Hopping mad and no relief in sight...

STRANGERS in Brynsiencyn are easily identified, and not just because it is a gossipy hen-coop of a place where practically the entire population is on more than nodding terms.

Visitors tend to stand out because of their curious gait, a half-walking, half-running shuffle in which the legs are frequently crossed. Often there is a suggestion of tears in the eyes. Another give-away is the frantic manner in which they bang on doors, scurry down alleyways or disappear behind hedgerows.

Such remarkable behaviour is commonplace in Brynsiencyn. Indeed, the whole village recalls the famous day when a coach load of old ladies gave a mass demonstration of it. Trading in the Half-Moon Stores came to an abrupt and noisy halt as the tourists hopped about with an agility which belied their years.

That odd episode, and many others, is very much part of the folklore of this Anglesey hamlet. It has put Brynsiencyn on the map. Why, even important people in remote Cardiff know all about it.

And about the day when an incredibly large Asian family trooped across the lounge of the Groeslon Hotel, leaving en masse 10 minutes later without buying so much as a single packet of curry-flavoured crisps.

Whether or not Brynsiencyn's rarified atmosphere is to blame has not been established. But it is a matter of indisputable fact that on arrival, all visitors are stricken by a dire need to go to the toilet.

Since Brynsiencyn does not offer this basic facility, they become desperate and irrational. The rational solution - to build a public toilet - was arrived at as far back as 1957. The first brick has yet to be laid.

The trouble is that Snowdon is in the way. Or rather, so the anti-loo lobby has argued, the toilets would obscure that beautiful sleeping mammoth. At 3,560 feet, Snowdon is considerably higher than the world's tallest urinal - wherever that might be. But it's all a question of perspective.

Passionately in favour of siting the new plumbing on the car park opposite the Groeslon Hotel, author and broadcaster Ian Skidmore carried out a scientific experiment.

Visualising a building no higher than 12 feet, and using the principles of Euripides, he determined that the only way you could not see Snowdon was to lie on the pavement outside the pub with your head in the gutter.

Even in this divided community it is generally accepted that few people would go to these lengths in order not to see such a glorious view.

It is also agreed that since he is a good licensee, Richard Jones would not allow his customers to reach the state in which they would involuntarily adopt the supine position - in which case their interest in the landscape would be purely academic.

At any rate, this impressive evidence was one of the factors which last week persuaded a Welsh Office planning inspector to end a situation more than reminiscent of that classic French tale, Clochemerle.

Those familiar with Gabriel Chavallier's novel will recall Monsieur le Maire announced to the town clerk: "I want to build a urinal, Tafardel."

"A really fine idea," came the reply. "An idea worthy of a good republican, and altogether in keeping with the spirit of the party. Equalitarian in every sense and hygienic, too, as you so justly pointed out."

But Clochemerele-en-Beaujolais was divided by this bold idea, and much hilarious and cunning to-ing and fro-ing took place before the mayor won the day and the loo was opened to the strains of the town band.

So it has been in Brynsiencyn-en-Allied Breweries where, according to Mrs. Celia Skidmore, the opposition has been led by an alliance of Welsh nationalists and the White Raj - a reference to the English settlers.

The militant faction staged protest marches on the car park, led by an elderly lady brandishing a placard. Jones Plaid Cymru spoke at length during the public meetings. Jones the Pub talked of politics rearing its ugly head and of Plaid trying to make political capital out of a situation which had reached bursting point.

There was talk of asking the authorities to add 12 feet to the height of Snowdon, he said. One of the sore losers was scheming to add the word "No" to the car park's "P" sign.

Skidmore The Print is waiting for climbers to complain that the toilets are obscuring views of the Groeslon. The battle has been fought with the same inspired genius and vigour as in Clochemerle, he said. One of the delights of village life was that this could happen without bloodshed.

After the second of two public inquiries in three intense years, the local paper announced last week: "Sighs of relief as Brynsiencyn loos now get go-ahead." Jones the Pub is sceptical. He has a gut feeling that this White Raj might delay things for years by quibbling over the design and building materials.

The opposition was tight-lipped. Two memsahibs politely but firmly turned me away. You get the feeling that in Brynsiencyn, as in Mafeking, relief will be a long time coming.

20 October, 1976

Aberfan's cry: Let us forget

OUTSIDERS, and there were quite a few of us in Aberfan this week, could sense the uncomfortable feeling in the air. People were preparing themselves for an emotional ordeal, preparing to cope once again with an inner pain that is always sharper at this time of year.

We were there to mark the tenth black anniversary of that unspeakable disaster. But no-one wanted to talk to us. They have lived through that vile experience time and again. They have relived it for the reporters who got their earlier. They have had enough.

Time has taken the edge off the grief, but it has not dimmed the memory. It is October - does it really matter which year? - and the images come surging back.

Little figures waving goodbye, their last words painfully locked in the minds of those who were never to see them again. Now they hear the words again, as if it were only yesterday, and see again the freshly scrubbed faces smiling farewell.

And the old familiar pain, like a punch to the heart, returns.

We, the observers, see it in their eyes and feel uncomfortable with them. We are intruding on a tangible grief that rises to the surface very time the eye catches the school picture on the sideboard or mantelpiece.

They will never forget, and probably don't want to. But if they had to lose their children, 116 of them, they could have wished for a better, more dignified way. That is what they must live with, the memory of a horror incomprehensible to anyone who was not there.

Two million tons of black dust, formed by rain into a slimy mass, moved like an obscene monster to engulf Pantglas Junior School and swallow the generation inside.

The world was aghast, but not all the words and pictures, as graphic as they were, could truly capture the feelings of Aberfan that day, and every day that followed.

You had to be there to know. You had to see the sobbing men, up to their thighs in slime and tearing at the debris with their bare hands. You had to lose a child to know what it did to mind and heart.

They are still haunted by that surrealistic day, still wondering why it was their child that had to die. So they have erected a wall of silence. It will not ease the pain to go over it again.

The television crews went away without interviews. One from America had to make do with a couple of people not happy about the way the £1 million disaster fund had been spent.

That's still a sore subject for many and the community centre committee resolutely refuse to answer questions. In fact, they held a meeting to decide that they would talk to no-one. They don't like the Press and have more than once turfed local reporters out of their meetings. Even today, bitterness and controversy remain.

But the school has gone, as has the church that served as a temporary mortuary. A children's playground, a new church and the huge community centre stand as memorials to the dead.

And on the hillside, two lines of pristine white arches marking the tiny graves. Even for the detached it doesn't do to linger here.

Gone, too, are the coal tips that are normally a feature of every mining community. They had to go, though not without a struggle, and Aberfan is all the better for that.

But, again, the bitterness remains. If only people had listened when the warnings were given. If only it had happened half an hour earlier. If only...

They paid a terrible price for man's folly, but life must, and does go on.

There will be no special service or ceremony tomorrow. This year is no more significant to the bereaved than any other. But tonight, with lanterns and torches, they will climb the hillside to lay wreaths, just as they have done every year on the eve of the anniversary.

As usual there will be one from teacher Bill Evans, who lost his wife and two children. His wreath will be inscribed with the ages the children would have been today.

It will be a poignant time for Susan Maybanks, 19, miraculously rescued after being buried in the slurry. And for Dilys Khan, one of only eight children in her class to get out alive. She scrambled through a high window so shocked she did not know she had four broken ribs.

Billy Williams lost his son Keith and cannot help but wonder what the boy would have been like now. He launched himself into local politics to make sure that a similar disaster would never occur again.

He was one of those instrumental in forcing the authorities to get rid of the coal tips. They went to Cardiff and threw black slurry at the feet of the Welsh Secretary, George Thomas.

Everyone in Aberfan has a story to tell, if they would bring themselves to do so. But collectively they have decided enough is enough. The world may need reminding, but they don't.

4 June, 1989

Meeting her was my good fortune

IN THE LAST few days I've had the usual crop of mail from readers convinced that I am a retarded bigot on extended leave from Old Nick's rather warm domain. The perspicacity of some folk is quite staggering.

One North Walian ventured the opinion (humorously he said) that I was "a silly old bastard." Less of the "old", sir, if you don't mind. The remainder is, of course, open to free debate.

He is another who subscribes to the blinkered view that the world would be a better place were all homosexuals confined to a remote island. His final enjoinder was that I should make amends "by showing queers a clean pair of heels."

Not likely. It would be just my luck to meet up with a foot-fetishist.

A Welsh lady asked if I would teach her to write, which made me laugh. I'm still learning myself. There are basic rules, but the rest is down to compulsion, imagination, imagery and a book of synonyms.

Without those, you might as well take up painting by numbers. According to one author, the secret of the craft is to insert a blank sheet of paper into a typewriter then open up a vein. He also said: "What no wife of a writer can ever understand is that a writer is working when he's staring out of the window." I have long been on intimate terms with my window.

Anyway, this is by the by, since I also get some nice letters and this week had the rare treat of actually meeting a reader socially. It was a bit like being gently buffeted by a warm wind.

She used to be Madame Someone or Other, but gave up telling fortunes because three of her husband's clients died. She suspected they would and while three deaths in 100 consultations wasn't too bad, they were enough to make her quit.

Her clairvoyant gift was largely sought by women, most of whom had three things in common. Either they were having an affair, contemplating one or suspected their husbands of infidelity. How unnerving for we men.

Madame Something had also discerned that my mind was troubled which was why, as the sole manufacturer, she had been sending me Pink Clouds (trademark) over the hills from the remote Welsh village in which she lives.

She confessed to being naughty, wild and not a little mad. "I'm a lot like you," she added. I took this to be a compliment since there is much to be said for those with the aural acuity to pick up the beat of a different drummer.

"I suppose you've noticed that I'm a bit excitable," she said. Indeed I had. Her tumbling river of words was accompanied by extravagant gesticulations and as we walked along the street my arm received not a few accidental clouts.

She was delightfully different, even down to the admission that, although a regular reader, she never buys the Post. With his unspoken permission, she "steals" copies from a neighbouring farmer. Enterprising, if a little depressing, for our circulation manager. Still, just so long as she's keeping abreast of the minor classics.

Our talk turned to country life and we agreed that, for most people, it was an idealised fantasy that often went wrong once realised. It can be infuriating to find your pretty white cottage pock-marked by huge dollops of pig manure.

Muck-spreaders are indiscriminate machines with great hurling power. Neither is it pleasant to live for days with an odour definitely not created by Coco Chanel. My God, but it stinks.

It is nothing to find a stranger peering through your windows or inspecting the front door. I regularly had to chase off ignorant townies trespassing in pursuit of childish treasure hunt clues.

I was also to be seen daily pursuing the two remarkably fleet-footed pigs I bought to dig up all the bindweed which was strangling the garden. They had a great talent for escapology and much preferred the vegetable patches of my irate neighbours.

There was no gas, no shops, no public transport and no children of a suitable age for mine to play with. Snow and ice brought chaos because country lanes are never gritted and you could be trapped for days in a bad winter.

Country folk, more gossipy than a coopful of hens, are wary of newcomers but will not rest until they know the bulk of your biographical details. Then they become very helpful, readily identifying with the problems of living in comparative isolation.

They intensely dislike Habitat yuppies who try to ingratiate themselves by ordering "a pint of cooking" at the local and being patronising to men in worn corduroys and soil-caked boots. They will never be dragged out of a drift by a tractor.

It's not all fresh air, fun and barbecues on the patio. It's pig-muck, problems and passing cattle dealers making coarse suggestions to your wife as she sunbathes in the garden.

Perhaps, as Madame suggested, you have to be just a little mad to live in the real countryside.

24 December, 1985

I'll be at Kate's place

I WAS a mere 15-year-old stripling when I fell in love with Kate, a married woman with three strapping sons. It was entirely innocent. This was the affection of a lad for the surrogate mother who made me part of her family.

Her door was ever-open to a procession of her boys' pals, brought home to listen to jazz records or to shoot the breeze with Ted, her late husband. His heart matched Kate's and their hearth was the warmest place I ever knew.

When the Army dispensed with my services after nearly two years in Africa, it was to "Kate's place," as we called it, that I headed first. I should have been marching home, but the cadences of my mind led me elsewhere.

I had trodden the same route for years, but never more joyfully than during those Christmases my own schismatic kin were away for the holiday. My pathetically unsubtle hints were unnecessary. Kate would simply not allow me to spend the time alone.

It was not just the enveloping blanket of the close-knit family that was special. It was the exquisitely hedonistic experience of dipping one's spoon into a steaming dish of tradition that few people in this country have been privileged to savour.

The magic word was *anelini*, a first course that made us all salivate with delicious anticipation while relegating the noble turkey to second best. And no wonder. It costs a small fortune and two days of devoted labour to make. It is poetry in pasta, a once-a-year delight on which the people of Bardi - a village north of Milan - will tomorrow gorge themselves with uninhibited relish.

Bardi long ago gave birth to *anelini*, as it did to the splendid character of Armando Marubbi who arrived in Wrexham penniless and hungry for work in 1897. He did not hunger long, peddling his own ice-cream from a handcart until he had enough money to open the cafe which still stands today in Abbot Street.

With his walrus moustached and rust-coloured Harris tweed suits, Armando was larger than life. People still remember how, when he was nagged by toothache, he drank a few glasses of rum and gouged out the offending fang with a jack-knife.

He became a pillar of the community, but never forgot his roots. When he married Teresina, a girl from another village near Milan, Armando taught her how to make *anelini* so that every Christmas would be like the ones he knew in Bardi.

They had ten children, of whom Kate is one of the three survivors. She remembers how Teresina always missed Midnight Mass on Christmas Eve so that she could complete the final preparations of the magical *anelini*. It was that important.

Kate was about 14 when her mother became ill and it fell to her to produce the chubby dumplings which float and bob in a broth so rich it could resurrect a dead donkey. Now she's 75 and still performing the annual ritual.

Mrs Catherina Davies, as she is more correctly known, lives alone, but never lonely, at Tan-y-Dre, Wrexham. Her boys - Geoff, Mike and Colin - long ago fled the coop, but never missed a Christmas without *anelini*. We all went our separate ways, but I was the only one to suffer withdrawal symptoms.

Then, some years ago, good old Lady Fate intervened. I was showing my new wife around North Wales when we walked into the open arms of Mike, Kate's second son, and Mary, his life-loving spouse. An old friendship was rekindled and a new tradition born.

Every year since, we have travelled to Mold on Christmas Day to enact the great *anelini* rite. Kate passed on The Knowledge and, believe me, the people of Bardi would be proud of Mary. Bellisima, they would cry, just as we do.

There will be nine of us at table tomorrow, with the benign matriarch in the place of honour. The young ones will feast on a great dish while I gorge myself on happy memories. As Kate says, it just wouldn't be Christmas without *anelini*.

3 April, 1988

Easter with Edna, our inebriate auntie

I JUST KNEW it was going to be a bad day when, at 6 am one Easter morning, Edna put her sparrow's head around the lounge door and said, " It's a struggle to be born and a hell of a fight to die."

Ninety minutes later she crashed off a kitchen stool and I was forced to abandon my fight with 17 Across. Only then did I realise that she had been trying to climb rainbows, injecting huge slugs of scotch to propel herself toward the final frontier.

She had too much fuel aboard. What can you say to a 72-year-old alcoholic in such sorry and embarrassing circumstances? I opted for, "Let me help you up, you silly old bugger." You can say things like that to people you love.

"Aunt" Edna - who is related to my wife by mutual affection - is a self-confessed oddity who talks to railway engines and other inanimate objects (including me) even when sober. God made her and discarded the mould, knowing that the world could not cope with replicas.

The world got the weekend off and I had to cope, Mrs Williams making tactical withdrawals for which I might yet smack her fetching bum. Edna sat on the stairs, coddled in my jacket, broke her heart and let its contents all but drown me.

In the course of that harrowing day we joined hands - literally and metaphorically - and went on uncomfortable rambles to somewhere remarkably like Hades. Into the bargain, she also gave me hell for hiding the booze.

I've had happier Easters and could well have done without the emotional molestation. It's hard to reason with someone who keeps saying, "Oh Lord, please help me to die. No-one wants to empty themselves into nothingness."

I pointed out that God, like everyone else, was entitled to a Bank Holiday break. If she really wanted to die she could nip to the off-licence. If she wanted to please those who bleed internally for her, she could start by helping herself to get better.

She won't. I have since discovered that her insides are like a plate of spaghetti bolognese - a real mess - and that she has between two months and two years left in which to startle the populace. She does it so well.

I shall never forget the faces of those who watched in disbelief as she talked to the train at Lime Street. Observing the normal standards of BR service, the rolling stock remained mute while I laughed my head off.

It was fun, too, at the wildfowl reserve when we arrived at the very still natterjack pond. A shrill, but cultured, voice rent the air with, "Toadies, toadies, where are you? Come on out, let's have a look at you."

On the way to a cemetery she asked, "Do you know why the sun is shining?" Fusty old me suggested meteorological influences. "Don't be silly," she said. "It's because I'm going to say hello to my mother."

The darker, but equally enigmatic, side of her nature emerged when she was helping to wash up. "I like knives in the same way that I like people," she muttered. There was a codicil. "I love mankind - it's just people I can't stand."

Poor Edna. Her haunted past spilled down the stairs. A broken marriage, the death of her second husband followed by the painful demise of a man who might have eased the desperate ache of loneliness.

Between torrid times there was the death of an infant, for which she unjustifiably blamed herself. The most generous person you could meet, Edna does not have the charity to forgive herself.

There was also the estrangement from her elder daughter, for which she relentlessly persecutes herself. The slings and arrows of outrageous fortune have left a gregarious being in manically depressive solitude.

Now, the world looks better to her through the base of a tumbler whose contents she can barely taste. Edna is drinking an undiluted anaes-thetic to ward off the chilling interference of that fickle bitch we know as Fate.

I looked into those still lovely eyes, but all I could see was a soul preparing to quit its mortal home. Those maudlin mirrors reflected a sad desire to slip the choking leash of a life laden with misfortune.

The worst moment came when Edna, the inebriate woman, wrote a cheque for £100 and said, "Now give me a drink." I refused on the ground that she had forgotten to include a tip. There followed a dreadful row.

She was killing herself and executing sensitive bits of me. We are kindred spirits, curios who march to the beats of different drummers and get into awful trouble for speaking our minds. We know everyone else is out of step - even when we're wrong.

When she finally left (a day late) Edna said, "I'm frightened of that six-hour journey. I just can't make it without a drink." My battle was lost. The label on the bottle bore the legend, "Afore ye go." It was 9 am.

To plagiarise Damon Runyan, Edna is people. But sometimes, even the loveliest people can strum your heart-strings and play the most melancholy tune.

THE BOX

JOHN had a love-hate relationship with the television. He mostly hated having to watch it but got great satisfaction from writing about it.

With just a few words he was able to sum up the view of millions of people and even those who did not agree with him would invariably laugh at his scathing remarks in Saturday's Daily Post.

In reality, the whole concept of a television review column baffled him. Either you watched the programme, so knew what it was like or you didn't, so what did it matter? But John was a true professional and every Friday he made damn sure that what he turned out was always his best.

4 October, 1981

Brideshead rejoicing

WHAT a deliciously decadent week on the box. Brazen ostriches unashamedly, and comically, coupling for the cameras, a Pope with a naked blonde under his cassock, and whiffs of depravity among Oxford's dreaming spires.

Of the three, it was the least explicit - as is the case with all naughtiness - which turned out to be the most intriguing and captivating. *Brideshead Revisited (Granada)* was an outrageously expensive vintage wine, to be swirled against the palate for as long as possible, to be indulgently savoured and, later, to be salivated over.

It was a sumptuous all-round triumph of television. Chances are it will not attract the hordes who are happier with the banalities of *Crossroads* than with the coruscating dialogue of Evelyn Waugh. No matter. Granada will surely be able to wallow in its prestige for years to come.

As much as anything it was a triumph of casting. Anthony Andrews was totally believable as the "beautiful, golden boy", a child-like fop always toting a teddy bear.

A wonderfully astringent performance from John Gielgud and a monumental success for Nicholas Grace, making my skin crawl with his portrayal of the disgustingly overt, stuttering deviant Anthony Blanche.

The goings-on in the cloisters, the incipient homosexual affair between Andrews and Jeremy Irons - "naughtiness in the ranks of grave sins" - was redolent of the atmosphere in which Burgess and MacLean must have been suborned and seduced.

So beautifully was it filmed that you felt you were strolling about inside the pages of a 1920's photograph album. Tuesday nights are definitely booked up until Christmas, though I cannot be too sure about Wednesday after the first episode of *The Borgias (BBC 2)*.

Given the reputation of this dubious family, you wouldn't want them as neighbours. Even safely trapped inside the tube, it's questionable on this showing if you would want them in your parlour.

It was a definite struggle to keep up with the plots and to translate all that fractured English. You had only to close your eyes to imagine some tasteless comic doing a take-off of an Italian ice-cream salesman, who, at the drop of a hat, would burst into: "Just one Cornetto."

I would have been glad of a word processor mounted on the arm of the settee alongside a mini-computer to keep track of all the characters. No Russian novel ever had so many. With the promise of much wickedness to come, I shall watch again. But unless it improves, I shall assassinate the Borgias at the touch of a switch.

Killing was the subject of *Forty Minutes (BBC 2)* which examined, with enlightenment from the murderer himself, the hi-jacking of a bus at an American airport and the slaying of two people.

"I am not totally to blame for what happened," said Louis Robinson, a sailor, who was worried about a pending investigation into the theft of a chicken-feed postal order. He became so paranoid - he also had a history of drug abuse - that he started waving a gun about and disrupted thousands of lives for ten hours. The programme was ostensibly about the police hostage squad which eventually grabbed this pathetic nutter.

But it was also a statement about life in the land of the free. Last year, 10,728 American citizens had their lives abruptly snuffed out by handguns, a fact the programme did not mention.

Robinson was partly right. How could he be wholly to blame in a society which allows any unstable fool to buy weapons with the same ease you and I can buy fish and chips?

So much more refreshing to turn to the animal kingdom in *Wildlife on One*, a filmic essay on the life of the ostrich, aptly titled *The Impossible Bird*. Such an absurd creature, which runs with all the grace of an aged spinster in inhibiting underwear, though a great deal faster. It even contrived to look silly while making love, its great neck flopping about like a rubber periscope.

The hens lay eggs so tough a man can stand on them without breaking their shells. Fascinating, therefore, to see a tenacious Egyptian eagle doing a demolition job with small rocks. Few chicks survive the elements and their predators, and most end up being taken from their parents by more aggressive families into an ostrich crèche.

Life can be cruel on the African savannah, but at least there are no crazed Yankee sailors about.

12 March, 1983

Oops, there goes another one

IN *QED (BBC 1)* the screen was full of people hell-bent on warping cutlery by way of psychokinetic energy. In the kitchen my wife was proudly holding a cup whose former appendage lay shattered on the floor.

Since she had been performing this feat of molecular disturbance - "It just came away in my hand" - at least three times a week for several years, Uri Geller's party piece seems quite ordinary.

What distinguishes one from another is that Geller receives more publicity and is suspected of chicanery. As are all his disciples who feverishly strain to fracture spoons and forks with mentally-generated beams of white light.

It seems a lamentable waste of good eating irons, but scientists are entranced. And, as this haphazard programme demonstrated, they are also gullible. In America they got all excited about two metal benders who later confessed to having cheated.

They were planted by a rascally conjuror, James Randi, who is obsessed with destroying the Geller legend. He has devised a test - not too difficult for any self-respecting white light - which carries a 10,000-dollar prize. The loot remains unclaimed.

Randi, who has a penchant for heavy disguises at Geller bend-ins, says the spoons get a jolly good waggling before Uri stroked them to destruction. A metallurgical microscope seemed to confirm this theory.

But Uri's trick with a piece of Longleat silver, certainly not one of the wonders of Woolie's, was harder to explain away. On the other hand, he complained of hostile influences when his white light failed totally under stringently controlled conditions.

The conclusion to be drawn is that there is no conclusion to be drawn as yet. Genuine or false, you still end up with a load of useless implements.

There was evidence of metal fatigue in the final episode of *The Cleopatras (BBC 2)*. Having given Mark Antony access to her king-size Slumberland, that dreadful Ptolemy hussy withdrew her favours in order to extract a favour.

Tony's white light almost wilted his breastplate, so he obligingly knocked off her sister then resumed a torrid affair in which both their posteriors got top camera billing.

Willowly girls wearing naught else but Ptolemaic G-strings cavorted about while Tone and Cleo emulated Taylor and Burton - a situation which could only lead to disaster.

"I hope there's enough asps to go round," said the raddled Roman, manfully stemming his belly-laugh which should have properly followed such a terrible line. Anyway the reptile did its job before viewers flung themselves upon it in desperation.

That same emotion was the running theme in the excellent *Lifer (ITV)*, Rex Bloomstein's two-hour documentary about men and women facing sentences of ten or more years.

Its impact was all the more remarkable because it was without comment, depending entirely on the often articulate stream of consciousness of the prisoners. While it is impossible to forgive their crimes, they presented faces human enough to chip away at the cast-iron philosophies of the sternest hang 'em and flog 'em merchants.

Most could not even recall their evil actions, committed under the influence of drink or drugs or else spurred by mental aberrations beyond their control.

There was little self-pity, just a common despair that when they had finished their time they would be hollow automatons who had been neither helped nor educated.

More than one felt that death was preferable and deserved, and one man had even worked out his own system of euthanasia. It was grim, fascinating and disturbing, principally because it robbed you of your self-satisfaction as a law-abiding member of society.

Talking of automatons, Richard Clayderman turned up in *Shirley Bassey - A Special Lady (ITV)*. While his magic is not available in the shops, it doesn't show up much on television, either.

His appeal lies largely in a pair of misty eyes which would not be out of place in the head of a spoilt doting puppy. There was a strong impression that it was part of his contract to have the camera stare into them every few bars.

It clearly pays to advertise. Though not in the case of Burt Reynolds, who was featured in the feeble *Superstar Profile (ITV)* series. Burdened by fame and an irresistible allure for women, Burt said he was lucky enough to have friends who allowed him to be dull. There were many times when he needed to be dull. Pre-empting one's own thoughts, he added: "Like now."

No white light was visible, but it was enough to bend a whole canteen of cutlery.

4 June, 1983

Will the pain in Spain ever wane?

WATCHING television last week, I was reminded of William Faulkner's story about a man who witnesses the lynching of a negro. When he arrives home his wife accuses him of having been with another woman, such is the guilt and shame etched on his face.

My normally sinister visage must have looked something like that as I sat and squirmed through the deliberate and systematic torture of an animal at the hands of arrogant young men.

Baited, wounded and bewildered, its body shuddered and heaved in a fight for reserves of breath. A spreading red patch glistened on its black coat.

When finally it was subdued, a man stepped forward to plunge a steel spike into its heart. The animal's mouth dropped open to release a torrent of blood which shot forward at least a yard. Life draining fast, it shambled a few reflex paces before the lights of the world went out for the poor beast.

My own mouth dropped open and the words "Jesus Christ" came out. I was not taking His name in vain.

I was, of course, watching Spanish TV and the bull-fighting equivalent of Match of the Day. The Spaniards have a deeply philosophical argument to justify this "sport" so eloquently glorified by the stupidly macho Ernest Hemingway. It does not move me. Like Faulkner's character I felt diminished.

Back in civilised Britain, where Michael Foot was being gored and Denis Healey was doing his wild bull impressions, El Thatchero locked horns with El Dayo in the *Panorama (BBC 1)* ring.

After exchanging a few gentle veronicas, Sir Robin charged at Mrs T's deceptive cape and was pierced by a couple of banderillos. The blood started to flow and you could practically hear shouts of "Ole" from supporters of both as each strove for the moment of truth.

Sir Robin was determined to reach her soul, while she fully warranted the soubriquet conferred on her by the Russians. It was a prickly, mesmeric confrontation and you wondered if Maggie had deliberately forgotten that Day was knight, addressing him as "Mr" throughout.

There was a suspicion that irascible old Robin, who is not used to defeat was losing his temper. But when he caught her out on defence and her record on prescription charges, she was visibly shaken.

But she won, though the kill was not clean enough for her to be awarded one of Robin's ears. At the end he felt prompted to offer a mild apology, to which she replied, "Don't worry Mr Day, I can handle you." You were left with an intense feeling of relief that she wasn't your mother-in-law. She is no sugar butty.

A much gentler woman had her emotions stripped bare for all to see in *The Visit: A Mother for Malcolm (BBC 1).* I am not sure that we should have been allowed to see it, just glad that we were.

White-haired Hilda has spent her life consumed with guilt because she was pressurised into giving away her illegitimate baby son more than 30 years ago. We can only guess at the anguish she has since borne, wondering where he was and what sort of man he had grown into.

Then in stepped Mistress Fate, arranging a fortuitous meeting between Malcolm and a man bearing the same surname. Their relationship established, arrangements were made for him to meet the mother he had never known.

This, of course, should have been an intensely private moment, destined as it was to have all the makings of a first-class weepie. Desmond Wilcox somehow persuaded them to make it a public event watched by millions.

The reunion took place on a station platform and as you might expect, was a very wet occasion. There were floods of tears, many mis-timed kisses and introductions to Hilda's new daughter-in-law and grandchildren.

It was heartwarming, as indeed was the whole programme, though Wilcox was sometimes guilty of hitting Hilda with questions calculated to bring forth stifled sobs and guilty silences. It was a remarkable story to have been party to, but left you with an uneasy feeling that you had been caught reading someone's mail.

It did not help to tune into *Question Time (BBC 1)* on which dastardly Denis Healey confessed to having shot himself in the foot by bringing up the Falklands factor.

Cecil Parkinson wore the expression of an injured schoolboy, Bill Rodgers waffled ineffectually and Denis was . . . well, just Denis. You'd need to be a genius to tell which one could be believed and in the end my mind drifted back to Spain, where they also have lots of bull.

7 January, 1984

A travesty of rites and wrongs

IN THE SIXTH interminable hour of *The Far Pavilions (C4)* Princess Shushila was voluntarily barbecued on her husband's funeral pyre. This diverting Indian rite is known as becoming suttee, though had she become Sweep you would not have been the least surprised.

Luckily for her, this scene was one of the few which did not contain the makings of a snigger or even a jolly good hoot. There were times when it was difficult not to believe this travesty of M.M. Kaye's romantic novel was not being played for laughs.

Rosanno Brazzi's deathbed scene was so comically-bad as to imperil one's rib-cage, while John Geilgud's demise was calculated to send one tumbling from chair to floor. Dying from a bullet in the gullet and soaked in blood he murmured, "Jenks, see if you can find me a clean shirt."

Threatened by 1,000 or so murderous tribesman, Jenks was clearly better off seeking refuge on the roof than rummaging through the linen closet to oblige a corpse with an exaggerated sense of occasion.

Back on the ground where it was obvious the screaming invaders had not turned up for a game of footer, the aptly named Captain Wally tried to stem the seige by saying, "Get back, there's good fellows." This being a notoriously weak military tactic as well as absurd dialogue he, very properly, was also shot.

This was no great loss since the chap had a funny sense of priorities. Asked in an earlier episode why he had sentenced a soldier to 15 days detention he replied: "Two days for firing at a missionary, and 13 days for bad marksmanship, sir."

The hero, Ben Cross, copped off with Princes Annuli, played by the badly miscast Amy Irving. While ackowledging that "men are careless of their seed," she invited him to make love to her in a sandstorm. Maybe it was all that grit flying about but Ben's seed was more careless than she knew and he failed in his expressed intention of impregnating her.

In short, it was sumptuously dressed tosh suffering from a surfeit of ridiculously stiff upper lips and a script culled from the pages of Boys'

Own and Mills and Boon. "I need you, heart of my heart, much more than life itself," breathed Anjuli, overlooking the fact that one was pretty useless without the other.

Filmed in India and North Wales, the landscapes were often magnificent. As the happy couple, together at last, rode off over a familiar looking hill it was easy to imagine them settling in Bethesda and being more careful with Ben's seed.

Exotic locations, too, in *Whickers's World (BBC 1)* in which our host out-parodied his many parodists when taking us aboard the QE2 on a voyage from Tahiti to New Zealand.

As far as one could tell the passengers were either rich or filthy rich, the sort of company in which Whicker has been mixing for many years. Perhaps too many, because there was an ominous sense of *déjà vu* about the interviews.

Whereas he used to ask wealthy widows why they had their faces lifted or tucks put in their bottoms, this time he was asking why they went cruising. Serried ranks of septuagenarians all said they wanted to relax, have some fun and be pampered. "On the QE2 they do everything but burp you," joked a Beverly Hills widow. Since the trip was costing her £140,000, I regard this as singular omission.

The ennui induced by this line of questioning was relieved when everyone went ashore on a Polynesian island to be garlanded by pretty girls. Seizing the opportunity for a cheeky double entendre, Whicker remarked about the huddled masses yearning for a good lei.

He met a millionaire who had bought five books to read on board, but in three weeks had managed only one page. "I don't do anything, but I don't have time to do anything else," he said. Another spent hours below decks doing giant jig-saw puzzles, oblivious to the marvellous coastlines floating by.

As one woman said of her fellow passengers, they were "dullsville." And, in the end, so was the programme which marked Whicker's return to the BBC. There is only so much mileage to get out of old people on a 96-day binge, no matter how much is in their bank accounts.

My own appearance on television this week, as a juror in *Crown Court (Granada)*, brought home to me the power of the medium. A neighbour who has pointedly ignored me for years greeted me as an old friend; a lady in the off-licence asked if I were someone famous, and casual acquaintances telephoned to ask if I actually knew I'd been on the telly.

All this for a minor, non-speaking role acted out with all the aplomb of a lump of wood. The kindest remark made was I looked like Edward VII in his declining years. The unkindest that I should have spent the three previous days in Make-Up.

No matter, the experience demonstrated the lengths to which Granada go to ensure the authenticity of every single detail. Very impressive, if a somewhat long and bum-stiffening day.

After watching the first episode I concluded that I had something in common with Rosanno Brazzi. We both died badly.

3 March, 1984

ABC of a sick-maker

AS AN everyday story of two nuclear war survivors being either violently sick or else planting lettuces, *Z for Zachariah (BBC 1)* was S for Satisfactory. However, since these activities have only limited appeal even for hypochondriacs and gardeners, it soon became D for Dreary.

Not to be too churlish, it deserved a full set of 5.9 marks for technical merit. Seldom can there have been more realistic vomit and, at one stage, Anthony Andrews sported the best set of bleeding gums you are ever likely to see.

As his condition deteriorated so the make-up department rose to the occasion giving him the dreadfully gaunt looks and deathly pallor of one emerging from a long sitting of Liverpool City Council. In fact, it wasn't that serious - just a case of radiation poisoning.

The story, which was ever so S for Slow, was about a pretty young survivor of the holocaust cheerfully living off the land until Andrews arrived dressed as a bee-keeper and lugging what looked like a posh dustcart containing his air supply.

There followed a bold piece of television in which he stripped off and pointed his squelchy bits at the camera which must have been D for Disappointing for his many admirers. After plunging into a polluted stream he became ill and took to leaving trails of lime green porridge all over mid-Wales.

Taking a turn for the worse, the play then became G for Gloomy as he gave the girl a crash course in the symptoms of radiation sickness and proceeded to go down the tubes.

The viewer could have been forgiven for thinking he was going to die, so it came as a surprise when he became R for Randy and tried to rape her. Sex equality being all important, this gave Pippa a chance to demonstrate that she is also good at vomiting.

No longer pals, they ambushed each other with rifles until Pippa nicked Tony's suit and dustcart and disappeared in search of more companionable forms of life. All very I for Implausible.

Badly in need of L for Laughs, I profitably turned to *Spitting Image (ITV)* which is to television what a blood transfusion is to a haemophiliac. Savagely satirical and naughty in the extreme it will do more to upset politicians than a bus load of Arthur Scargill clones.

The amazingly manipulative puppets are grotesque but immediately recognisable, caricatures of the famous. The voices are uncannily good and the script has the cutting edge of a diamond, even if it occasionally strays into the realms of bad taste.

An early sketch had John McEnroe's voice screaming from a blanked out screen. "It was in, I tell you. It was definitely in." The lights went up to show him in bed with Joan Collins, who told him he'd been nowhere near. Ayatollah Khomeini was seen using the index finger of a severed hand as a pen.

Also near the knuckle was Ronnie Reagan coupling with Nancy and asking if the earth had moved for her, too. Since it hadn't, he reached out and pressed a bedside button marked, "Nuke." Ian Paisley tore a strip off God for tolerating Roman Catholics and Mrs Thatcher was seen in Buck House calling out, "I'm ready to see you now, Ma'am."

A host of other characters were lampooned and lambasted in quick succession, none more hilairously than Comrade Chernenko who dropped dead in the Kremlin and was worked from behind by a couple of Brezhnev look-alikes to convince the public he was still alive. Shades of the barely-cold Andropov.

It was with U for Unease that I approached *The Other Half (BBC 1)* in which novelist Sir Angus Wilson discussed his 32-year relationship with his "secretary", Tony Garrett. Not because of their homosexuality, rather the Peeping Tom nature of the series.

Not to worry, it was as unremarkable as have been the others simply because the couples instinctively know where to draw the line. In any case, personal revelations would be embarrassing for subject and viewer alike.

Angus is 70, has the face of an aged elf and a mouthful of teeth like well-spaced, discoloured tombstones. Tony is 55 and handsome and lost all interest in girls when, as a boy, he discovered they wore lumpy knickers.

They flit from party to party being witty and popular, live in perfect harmony and can never conceive of the time when they will not be together. Which is more than can be said of many heterosexual unions.

The unfairly talented John Mortimer turned up on *Wogan (BBC 1)*, which could be a sign that Terry is struggling for new faces. Devotees of chat shows will be so familiar with Mortimer as to feel entitled to be invited to his place for Christmas.

Victoria Principal did a sales pitch for her book which advocates changing the way we live, starting by being beautiful on the inside. Which probably means eating bran and prunes and going to the toilet regularly.

All standard chat show stuff. It's a good job Wogan has the wit and wisdom to make the majority of his guests seem more interesting than they really are. Definitely C for Clever.

10 March, 1984

Don't laugh.... it's drama

IT WAS just another ho-hum day in Denver. Blake was lying unconscious on a mountain, Cecil was lying in an oxygen tent while Alexis was merely lying. Fallon's baby was kidnapped, the nannie had a police record, Claudia was going quietly bananas and the Carringtons' long lost son had turned up after 25 years.

Is it stretching a point to suggest that the family is going through a bumpy patch? Will we next discover that Blake's grannie is a hitman for Mothercare or that Krystle leads a secret life as a hod carrier?

Do not scoff. In *Dynasty (BBC I)*, absurd scenarios breed like over-sexed bunnies. The cast is doomed to lurch from one manufactured crisis to another until the script writer is gently led away by men in white coats murmuring: "Jelly for tea."

Poor old Cecil had a massive coronary after going to bed with Alexis (Joan Collins), which was probably due to seeing her without make-up and noting that her cheeks are caving in. With just 24 hours to go to their wedding, it was rather extreme as subterfuges go.

But even inside his plastic bag, his face a delicate shade of grey tinged with blue there was no escape from the mercenary Joan, cruelly referred to in Hollywood as the British Open. With *rigor mortis* apparently two gasps away, she was desperate for the nuptials.

At this point the writer dithered, clearly not knowing how an English woman would make an impassioned plea. He settled for: "Let this union that was meant to be take place now," which was fairly near the mark, had it been said in the 18th century.

Unsure of his ground, he next had her say: "We've got beautiful things to do together." One of those things having led to his demise, Cecil parted his dry lips in a manner which suggested that he was more prepared to meet his maker in heaven than Joan at the altar, or next to the oxygen cylinder, as it would have been.

As lip movements go, it was great acting. . .

You might laugh, but in America patients at death's door are allowed to have gold diggers propose to them through the flaps of their life support systems. Honestly. As true as I am sitting on this camel.

Dynasty takes to extremes the Greek premise that all drama stems from conflict. Indeed, it often relegates Greek tragedy to the realms of Mrs Dale's Diary, whose pages frequently deflected me from a comforting cup of Earl Grey and a gipsy creme. I'm a sucker for sadness.

But I also like a good laugh and am given to hysterics which have led me to be shamefully expelled from church and amiably ousted from a union meeting. This week I was convulsed by *Ice Hockey Night (ITV)*, in which a goal-tender, as they are quaintly called, was criticised by the commentator for failing to keep his skates together when the puck was flashed towards him.

This weakness allowed the other side to score six goals and prompted the indiscreet observer to remark: "He's having a lotta trouble between his legs." Which led me to wonder why he was picked for the team in the first place.

Still, it makes a change from boring soccer, disastrous cricket in Pakistan, phoney wrestling and international rugby blatantly rigged to deprive Wales of the Triple Crown. Who changed the rules to allow other teams to win?

Obviously some chauvinistic swine like Ronald Merrick who continues to sneer his nasty way through the compelling *Jewel In The Crown (ITV)*. God, how I'd like to beat him over the head with his false arm, and rip his baggy shorts to shreds.

This, of course. is a tribute to the acting of Tim Piggot-Smith as the officer who hates coloureds, ex-public schoolboys, fellow officers and memsahibs who couple with Indians. He is the ultimate Bigot-Smith.

The series has always been languid in pace, but never less than intriguing because of the continuous threat linking it to explosive opening episodes when the affair between Daphne Manners and Hari Kumar came to its tragic end.

It is certainly stronger on dialogue than action, and the lifting of an eyebrow often speaks volumes. It has so far been a brave and rewarding production for anyone prepared to listen. This week's duel between Major Merrick and Sergeant Perron was mesmeric.

"Are you one of those who believe that if you teach an Indian the rules of cricket, he will become an English gentleman?" leered Merrick. "Certainly not. I know some Englishmen who play cricket brilliantly who are absolute shits," retorted Perron.

He was obliquely referring to Merrick and all those Brits who regarded India as their gin and tonic playground; a place where the plumber was automatically elevated to the rank of sanitary inspector and behaved like the Minister of Health.

Fresh Fields (ITV) is a new sit-com in which a middle aged wife seeks to ginger up her life. Her husband sits behind the Financial Times saying: "Mmmm," in all the wrong places, her mother lives next door and the other neighbour is an engaging scrounger.

Everything she undertakes comes to naught. Everything she says is misunderstood.

Asked if their daughter is still living in sin, she replies: "No, Pinner." I think I've seen it before. Many times.

11 December, 1982

Brookside, where the air is blue

IN *CINEMA 82 (BBC 1)*, the colourless Iain Johnstone described wrinkled celebrity ET as "a deliberately ugly little bugger." What slander! To my certain knowledge, Speilberg's creation is not even suspected of unnatural sexual proclivities.

Johnstone was not, of course, suggesting anything of the kind. He was probably trying to be a little daring to counteract the soporific effect of a voice almost totally devoid of inflection.

His misuse of the word, though not offensive, was indicative of current trends to bring broadcasting down to street level. There is a misguided belief that the boringly repetitive expletives of the ignorant can be equated with realism.

In a sighting almost as rare as water buffalo in Bootle, Phil Redmond turned up on *Exchange Flags (Granada)* to defend the woefully limited vocabularies of his Brookside characters.

With breathtaking arrogance, he asserted that were they not foul-mouthed he would be cheating the audience and belittling their intelligence. Realism was his goal.

He is guilty on both counts. The audience, such as it is, is getting a distorted view of Merseysiders. Millions whose intelligence was insulted have turned off.

His next statement, equally as startling, was that there are sections of the community who want their children introduced to bad language to prepare them for life.

Hopefully he will forgive me for not applauding this valuable public service. And for failing to perceive this drama as an instrument of education.

Perhaps in years to come a young man will appear on *University Challenge* and say "Patrick O'Hooligan, Magdalene College, reading the Humanities and Brookside. So....off, Bamber."

In the face of biting criticism, Mr Redmond remained perched atop

Olympia. It took a taxi driver in the studio audience to put it all into perspective.

"If it wasn't for the swearing, Brookside would be instantly forgettable." So spake Mr Average, who won't be cheated or have his intelligence belittled.

Four-letter words were so prevalent in *The Stable Lads Night Out (40 Minutes, BBC 2)* that the use of the bleeper began to sound like an extended message in Morse code.

This was a savagely cynical sketch of racing society at its worst, exposed by an excess of booze as being well-heeled yobs and snobs.

The occasion was a dinner to support the Stable Lads' Trust, whose declared aims are to look after the education, welfare and recreational needs of their charges.

The camera was merciless. You watched the owners and trainers becoming progressively drunk, foolish and objectionable as they flashed £5, £10 and £20 notes with obscene ostentation.

Their antics were contrasted with the lives of three lads put out of work by illness or injury, and one who committed suicide, who received not a penny from the Trust.

Meanwhile, their patrons were splashing out £100 a time for draw tickets for a Rolls Royce. Two Hooray Henry's paid £1,200 for a Botham cricket bat, which they proceeded to ruin by smashing at champagne bottles.

The lads earn £73 a week before deductions. The Trust's assets are £431,000-plus. Last year it doled out £569 for the poor and sick. Its administration expenses were £35,000.

There was no doubt the programme was outrageously slanted, but with obvious justification. No wonder the Trust wanted it withdrawn and refused to be represented.

The imminence of Christmas is always marred for me by the TV commercials. Promoting his cheap splash-on scent for men, Henry Cooper has this year been joined by Barry Sheene and his bird, who is to singing what I am to bra modelling.

But more irritating is the return of the obnoxiously good-looking Frenchman, oozing sexual innuendo as he pours a liqueur for that patently Slack Alice Englishwoman.

He always elicits longing sighs from a certain person is our house. Only an heroic effort of self-restraint prevents me from adding to Brookside's rich dialogue.

15 December, 1984

Acid-drops rain forest

I HAD ONE of those Sunday lunches known in the office as "a First Division match." Which is to say that it began at 1 pm and tapered off six hours later with the problems of the world sorted out and the grape growers of Tuscany considerably better off.

Before drifting off into a reverie I had only a misty impression of *The Ebony Tower (ITV)*. An old man enjoying himself, lots of trees and Toyah Wilcox's admirably formed bum. "You missed nothing," reported an equally Tuscanied colleague who had kept his eyes open.

The big nit. As I discovered the following day, it was gorgeous. Which man did not have the urge to tear off his thermal underwear and frolic in the sun-shafted forest, or splash in the mirror lake with those nubile, nude girls?

Which myopic viewer was not captivated by ravishing landscapes which were ravished by the camera in the manner of a skilled lover making his partner purr with pleasure?

The old man was the old master Laurence Olivier, up to his bushy eyebrows in the sheer delight of creating the combative, crusty old artist spitting on the critics and "like the old Romans, suckling the milk of young girls for strength."

"We don't deny him the little bit of love life he can still manage," Greta Scacchi told the visiting young painter (Roger Rees) giving him a close-up of eyes which could detach the braces from your trousers across a crowded room.

You could almost hear Roger's elastic snapping as the sexual tension between them built up. She was eager for dalliance but, in the event the boff was off, leaving a frustrated Roger to take yet more wicked baiting from the old man.

The verbal exchanges, if sometimes esoteric, were delicious sugar-coated acid drops and Toyah popped in and out of the action like some exotic punkish creature you would expect to find under a spotted toadstool. It was splendid.

The Secret Servant (BBC I) ended with a cry of anguish. It was mine. With not a drop of Tuscany's finest to zap the old brain-box, I remained bemused. After all that international espionage bit, it boiled down to someone having devoured someone else in the desert about 40 years ago.

For all the entertainment it gave over three nights, it might as well have been distilled into a five-minute slot on cannibalism in the Food and Drink programme. I suspect it was appreciated only by those who felt velvety fingers up and down their spines when Charles Dance was in camera.

Hardly anything new emerged from *A Tribute to John Lennon (ITV)* in which a slightly pretentious American commentary tried to build him up into something more than just a gifted tune-smith.

Indeed, much of it was devoted to Yoko who, with her talk of suffering and struggling as an artist, appears to be afflicted with a bad case of art in the head. But, at least, Paul McCartney was graceful enough to admit that she had been misjudged and was not the virago we all thought.

What was comical, and alarming, was the revelation that the FBI wasted three years investigating the Lennons in the hope of deporting them. And a letter to the White House described them as a threat to national security. What a funny lot the Yanks are.

In both senses of the word, since *The Betty White Show (C4)* was the funniest thing on the box all week. Part of Channel Four's celebration of Mary Tyler Moore's production company, it is one import I would really welcome.

The gag-a-minute humour stems mainly from the venomous bitchery between a divorced couple forced to work together. "Oh, you've grown a moustache. Or did you have anchovies for lunch?" says Betty to the wickedly droll John Hillerman.

Explaining why she now has a female companion: "After you left I felt the need for another human being around. Come to think of it, that's how I felt when you were here."

My favourite line was when she told her friend: "The most romantic thing he ever said to me was: 'Am I too heavy?'" I think she stole that one from my wife.

26 April, 1986

Enemy at the door maybe

AN ALSATIAN dog tried to buy my house last week. I assumed this to be the case because it left a large deposit on the doorstep. Its owner was a model of restraint, waiting patiently until the mutt furthered its practical studies for an Open University degree in domestic hygiene.

In a state of nakedness in the bedroom, I tried to register disapproval without giving the impression that I was the neighbourhood's resident pervert. There must have been more of me showing than I realised, because my window banging brought a cheery smile and wave in response.

Owners are generally oblivious to the offence their pets cause, and you are forced to conclude they would only get the message if a dog warden entered their homes and officially despoiled the living room carpet.

A Wolf In Dog's Clothing (Q.E.D., BBC 1) admirably demonstrated the unfettered loopiness of those who believe pooches come before people. The sort who see their Doberman at someone's throat and chide, "No supper for you tonight, Franz, you naughty boy."

There was Robert Tuckman whose Old English sheepdog shared his bed, went to the office with him and ate lunch with the staff. A lovely animal whose single vice was that he frequently sank his fangs into the long suffering Mrs Tuckman.

Understandably - and unlike her husband - she could not bring herself to think of Sam as a brother and surrogate son. Bob returned one day to find the dog had been put down. His wife is now the former Mrs Tuckman and another sheepdog is shedding hairs on the bed linen.

Then there was the entrepreneur who firmly believed no woman wearing designer clothes and accessories would be seen dead with a pet not similarly attired. Incredibly, scores of people agreed and she made a fortune dressing up dogs like dogs' dinners. "Simple leather shoes are not good enough," she said.

It was unconvincing to the boy who needed six hours of surgery after being savaged by three bull terriers. It was of no interest at all to the woman who bled to death after a similar attack. She hardly noticed the footwear or the diamond choker.

It emerged that dog owners felt aggrieved if people did not like their pooches. They took it as a personal criticism. This was heartening news since the rest of us firmly believed they were as dumb as the creatures who dump tons of crap on our streets and parks.

Top Gear (BBC 2) went to the Turin motor show to look at phallic symbols, ego boosters and bird-pullers which in a few years will be carefully clocked and bodged by your friendly neighbourhood second-hand car dealer.

I shall never forget the thrill of inserting the key into the door of my Italian sports car and watching in fascination as it withdrew the lock barrel to the accompanying musical shower of hundreds of rust flakes.

And how vivid is the memory of hamlet folk exclaiming, "John Williams passed through here today," while feeling for each other in the pall of oily smoke left by my second Italian sports car. I was the greatest forecourt sucker of all time.

I was in tucks at the story of Spike Milligan taking a taxi all the way from Finchley to central London to whack a stage doorman who had put down the phone on him. It was funny, yet symptomatic of the man's neuroses.

He once threatened Peter Sellers with a knife. The worried comedian bought a book on self-defence which Milligan found and hit him over the head with. Hilarious, but yet another illustration of the dark side of a laughter-maker who is crying on the inside.

Spike (C4) was a fascinating profile of an acknowledged comic genius who bleeds internally for mankind, children and animals and spends long periods in black depressions. In this programme he exhibited all the *joi de vivre* of an undertaker on a day when no-one died.

He considers himself the leper of light entertainment and is thought to be inspired, dangerous and a hit-and-miss performer. His moods are mercurial and he would gladly kill those who wronged him, particularly the nuns who educated him. But is he serious? Only mad Milligan knows.

The same channel also paid tribute to *Eric Bristow: Arrogant, Irresponsible Genius* for his prowess at throwing little feathered friends at a lump of cork. Even his mother agreed he had a big head.

This may be due to his intake of lager as much as his ego, since his face is bloated and he has as many chins as the Hong Kong telephone directory. A darts fanatic since the age of 11, he has all the depth of a Kleenex tissue - plus a million quid.

He exudes the self assurance of a Cockney, which immediately brands him as a nose blocker, runs an appalling club and is universally hated by darts fans. In other words, he is immensely successful.

A genius he is not. A consistently accurate thrower of flighted missiles he most certainly is. If that meagre talent is rated to be worth a million by today's standards, you can hardly blame the bloke for being arrogant. Just compare him to all the drongoes who shell out to watch him.

14 March, 1987

Anyone for jam and crumpet

DAGMAR O'CONNELL looks deceptively normal but, I ask myself, has she been correctly wired up? There must be serious doubts about a woman who actively encourages the use of jam, jelly, feathers and water colours in love-making.

You might think that Dagmar - who owns the stickiest duvet in America - is in need of expert help. Forget it. She is the expert help. Her job is to pep up the sex lives of couples married to each other forever.

I fear the effect on the average woman seeing her ageing husband entering the bedroom with a jar of Hartley's and a sheaf of feathers. She might suspect the marriage had broken down and she was about to be run out of town on a greasy pole.

Dagmar's novel uses for these basic commodities were not divulged when she appeared on *Daytime (ITV)* for a studio debate on her succinctly titled book, *How to Make Love to the Same Person for the Rest of Your Life - And Still Enjoy It*.

One couple took her advice and staged an afternoon picnic with smoked salmon sandwiches and a bottle of bubbly. They got crumbs everywhere, wet the bed (so to speak) and broke the glasses. "You should see my knees. It was acutely dangerous and sordid," the man complained.

Claire Rayner, whose blouse was fighting a losing battle with her chest, was also a proponent of food on the nuptial couch. "It doesn't have to be expensive, though," she said. "You can do just as well with fish paste."

Claire has what is politely known as a fuller figure. It was difficult to imagine Mr Rayner shipwrecking in the billowing whiteness of her thighs while nibbling a paste butty and trying to keep the jelly steady. "Did the jam move for you, too, darling?"

Molly Parkin tried to keep the romance in her marriage (one of them) by taking her husband off to an hotel to see how many times they could couple in 24 hours. The poor bloke managed eleven and a half sorties, but she still divorced him. I expect he's now in a home for the disabled.

Molly, wearing what appeared to be a small shrubbery, was only one of several people who didn't mind revealing intimate details of their private lives.

It was left to a homely old soul to put the whole matter in perspective. "The flames might die down, but it's important to have a warm lap to put a cold bum into at night," she said. The insatiable little spitfire.

If discussions like these are becoming franker, it also seems that comedy is getting coarser. In the opening monologue of *The Bob Monkhouse Show (BBC 2)* our hero told a gag about a Joan Collins doll coming on the market. "Whenever it sees an Action Man, it lifts up its nightie."

Michael Bentine said how much of Shi-ite was the Ayatollah, referred to the homosexual preferences of some MPs and sailors, then produced a ghastly puppet vulture which proceeded to do a prolonged, simulated pee all over the place.

I'll have trouble forgiving *BBC 2* for *Dead Head* which turned out to be a dead loss, even as a vehicle for writer Howard Brenton's apparent dislike of royalty, aristos and the police.

In his search for the murderer, Eddie Cass bumbled into yet another piece of high class crumpet who just couldn't resist a bit of rough. Before you could say jam or jelly they'd locked limbs in what turned out to be a totally irrelevant scene.

Later, some highly placed government official told Eddie that the maniac was a member of the royal family, hence the cover-up. As you know, arrogant mandarins are always giving away state secrets to petty crooks.

Not only that, they bunged him a fortune with which to buy an hotel in the Bahamas in exchange for his silence. The final scene lacked only a herd of pink elephants and airborne pigs to make it absolutely convincing.

In *The Marriage (BBC 2)* - such a dreary series - the stupid, feckless Marc went on a rugby trip to Scotland and spent a lot of time with an old flame who was built like a semi-detached house. For some strange reason, his new wife was hacked off.

As an act of penitence, he allowed himself to be interrogated about his indiscretion by Desmond Wilcox. For his own sake and ours, he should have taken his medicine and spared us the tedious confessional.

Des did everything but don cassock and mitre, conveniently forgetting that his own indiscretion led to divorce and eventual marriage to Esther Gleem-O-Dent. But that's showbiz.

22 July, 1989

Glorious Gaynor brings out the Latin in me

OH, GOD. I fear I have fallen victim to pre-senile dementia. When you get hooked on *Come Dancing (BBC 1)* you know that there is something terribly wrong with whatever is masquerading as your mind.

I blame it all on those figure-hugging costumes and the sequins. And don't some of the women look nice too - all those libidinous legs and faces like traffic mishaps.

Chiefly, though, I blame Gaynor Fairweather, whose name is only marginally less unfortunate than having been christened Gladys Goodbody. It would have been more appropriate, since the frame of this dame is the stuff of which restless nights are made.

Gaynor is one half of the World Latin American champions and when she smiles it's like staring straight into the grille of a 1950s Buick. Her make-up would support a sizeable building, but what a mover.

Her partner, Donny Burns, dances the role of the lounge lizard to perfection. Together they personify outrageous exhibitionism and, let it be said, erotic artistry which reminds you of the days when your hormones actually worked for a living.

They are demonstrably professional and exciting. It must be a hell of a comedown to be part of the Penge Formation Team and follow an act which could irremediably corrupt a geriatric monk.

Such an unworldly being would be in no danger from Annabel Croft, failed tennis player and surrogate derrière for the vomit-inducing Anneka Rice. Now hosting *Interceptor (ITV)* she was living proof of how the world can be unjustly generous to the talentless.

At 60 minutes the show was approximately 58 minutes too long, but would still have been an insult to the intelligence of the average moron. I was terribly insulted.

Some friends in the business of probation and social work kindly recorded for me *Hard Cases (ITV)*. We settled down to watch and after

15 riveting minutes one of the trio went to bed and the other took me to the pub. It was really good.

Then on Thursday I had a terrible accident. Caught unawares in the middle of crippling torpor I watched *People (BBC 1)* and was paralysed by its awfulness. Is there not some charitable foundation which could protect Frank Bruno from himself?

Better still, is there not one which could safeguard others from BBC personnel labouring under the misapprehension that they were correctly wired up at birth and know exactly what amorphous masses want?

Frank caused grievous bodily harm to Her Majesty's native tongue, laughed like Boris Karloff in a wicked role and communicated with the ease of an arthritic night watchman on a Jane Fonda aerobics course.

One of his guests was a little girl whose ambition was to marry a rich man whom she could divorce and then take to the cleaners. As little girls go, she was unadulterated arsenic and old face. I expect her mother's a disillusioned nun with at least one bad habit.

Really absorbing was *Lord of The Golden Triangle (ITV)* which was all about the man who runs the biggest heroin operation in the world. He even has a 20,000 strong army to keep at bay the Americans and Burmese troops.

He claimed to be simply a politician working to liberate an oppressed people. Personally, I thought he was trying to amass enough cash to give his parents a decent wedding. Even if I'm right, he'll always be a bastard.

In *Shadow of The Cobra (BBC 1)* Art Malik played a man with honey in his eyes and stones in his heart. By occupation he was a mass murderer, a skill not yet included in the YTS range of career options.

It was good because Malik's role demanded that he had the intellect of Wittgenstein and the charisma of a Hollywood actor, most of whom think that intellect is about overseas phone calls. He was manipulative and seductive, almost convincing investigative journalists that only the Pope was slightly purer than he.

There now follows two public announcements. Firstly, I'm going away to gorge myself on Pavarotti and trashy novels for a fortnight.

Secondly, there is an apology to a writer who thinks my sense of humour is detached from reality. I cannot disagree. If one is to be detached from anything, what better starting point could there possibly be?

4 November, 1989

Maggie danced, while Brian called the tune

IF YOU wanted the replay of St George & The Dragon, all you had to do was to tune into *The Walden Interview (ITV)* at the unnatural hour of 1 pm on Sunday. Mrs Thatcher was good, Brian Walden was wonderful.

He put her on the rack with a dogged persistence which had even me, a seasoned pro, squirming. She tried all the tricks in her personally autographed book but Walden kept nipping at her ankles like a dyspeptic Jack Russell terrier, and you know how cantankerous those little sods can be.

Brian earnestly wanted Mrs T. to confess why she had not sacked Professor Walters in order to keep Nigel. The answer seems obvious, but the Iron Lady did a merry dance that made you want to hug her warmly round the throat.

I'm enjoying writing this, if only to confound those bigots who firmly believe I am in the pay of Conservative Central Office. Yaa, boo and sucks to you. I'm a free man who doesn't pander to anyone as low as a politician.

Anyway, Mrs Thatcher gave a good account of herself and said she likes a good argument, which is a fail-safe way of discovering the tendentious opinions of one's opponents. They are only tendentious if they disagree with you.

However, during this arresting programme, a fulsome tribute was made to Mrs Thatcher as being "sweet and reasonable". Since the words fell from her own lips, we were allowed a generous pinch of salt. I hope my critics will now be sated.

On *Wogan (BBC 1)* Katie Boyle, from whom I recently received a lovely letter, confessed to all about her breast surgery and said her husband had lost two really good friends. She was nothing if not frank.

I happen to love her and feel I have lost three good friends. On the same programme was an American woman who had endured plastic surgery to her eyes, nose, lips, stomach and had her fat sucked out through her navel. I didn't actually see it, but the navel was probably her best feature.

I wanted to watch Alan Ladd in F. Scott Fitzgerald's classic story, *The Great Gatsby*, but was told by a faceless voice that it had been transferred to November 16. How very BBC 2, which seems currently obsessed by snooker and bowls.

Sport is so awfully boring, and only briefly diverted by the trim, white-skirted bum of a bowler by the name of Margaret Johnston.

She was superb, and although I did not see the end of the match, I hope she won. Her figure deserved a victory.

I watched *The Les Dawson Show (BBC 1)* and thought how he filled the bill as an alternative comedian. He unmercifully extracted the urine from David Essex, who now has come-to-bed eyes with his own pillows under them, "Your songs kept us going through the Blitz," Les told him.

I didn't get the one about the woman with a sack of wheat on her back who was looking for an all-night windmill, and didn't care for the one about the woman who fell in a jelly and was set for life.

Did you see *Mother Love (BBC 1)* ? Wasn't Diana Rigg delicious as the possessive bitch with an overpowering love for the son she referred to as Kitten? She was regal, serene and thoroughly nasty. Pure acid. It reminded me of the Walden Interview.

The dialogue was as catty as a pets' home and we were looking at the other side of an Oedipus complex. I haven't had so much fun since granny fell on the fire. It was wonderful.

Inside the Brotherhood (ITV) was about men who roll up their trouser legs and take solemn vows of verisimilitude in case their willy drops off. Or something like that.

It was all about Freemasons, brotherly love, charity and how it's almost impossible to get a fiver out of them unless it's for the Grand Lodge. They were accused of ruining businesses for those who did not toe the line.

I think there is something sinister about them, and all policemen should be banned from membership. After all, who wants a bobby who is prepared to roll up his trouser legs for another man? The silly madam.

11 October, 1986

Burning with a devilish revenge

DID YOU see the haunches on that gigantic wench in *The Life and Loves of A She Devil (BBC 2)*? Granite crushers. And those amazing mammaries, either of which could do untold damage if carelessly dropped on one's foot.

It came as no surprise to learn that they are to star in a new James Bond movie in which they are deployed to crush the life out of an enemy agent. What a way to go - boobed to death in the course of duty.

Julie T. Wallace cuts a remarkable figure with her clothes on. Nude she is staggering, a colossus with everything a man could want - muscles, a moustache and a couple of fetching warts appended by the make-up department.

Hers was an acting debut with impact, physically and theatrically. Too big to attend the Ugly Bug Ball, she imposed her formidable presence on this scarcely credible tale by Fay Weldon. If looks could kill, undertakers everywhere would be doing a joyful jig.

She played the wronged wife of Dennis Waterman, who busied himself by offering financial advice to a rich bitch while joyfully shipwrecking in the billowing whiteness of her thighs. A versatile little chap.

His wife fretted, brooded and glowered, shooting him glances that would turn milk into yoghurt before it had left the cow. He finally left her for the bitch, who was also being serviced by her butler. Who says you can't get decent help anymore?

Slightly miffed, the Amazon burned down the family home, plonked the kids on Dennis and went starkers to exploit the alchemy within her with which she will make her husband's life a sheer misery. Sounds like the average scorned woman. Keep watching.

To be absolutely fair to Edwina Currie, she comes across as an arrogant, patronising prat. Her views on Northern living habits are, in general, quite right. Her delivery was less than tactful and she deserved the plague of fleas in her ear.

Despite the evidence to prove her point, *World In Action (Granada)* practically looped the loop in its efforts to score off the Tory party. At one point the interviewer was reduced to scolding her for not recognising that poor people needed cigarettes to get through the day.

They produced a couple who could not afford fruit for the children, but who both smoked. At a conservative estimate their habit represents £20 a week. That's a lot of apples and pears or a whole heap of cancer, whichever way you look at it.

Other poor people were seen sitting in clubs surrounded by empty pint glasses. The interviewer railed against Mrs Currie while the film shored up her case. Like the *She Devil*, the programme was full of boobs.

Talking of which brings me to Pam Ewing, one of the best jigglers in the business, who got married in *Dallas (BBC 1)* then found her former dead husband taking a shower. In a full explanation of his absence, Bobbby said "Hi." Very convincing.

The plan is that he will either be another long-lost relative or that Pam will awake from a bad dream. The series starts again this month with an invitation to the terminally bewildered to watch while strumming their fingers across their lips and making strange sounds.

Ever attuned to public taste, the Beeb has begun a new series of *The Muppet Show (BBC 1)*. While this enables me to continue my vicarious love affair with Miss Piggy, it enrages the tinies in our house.

It's not that they mind me being unfaithful to Mummy with an egotistical sow, they want to get in on the act. But 7.35 pm is well into "snuggle down with teddy" time and just on the fringe of peak viewing for odd blokes who like temperamental pigs.

It is a strange example of scheduling. The little persons who most want to watch Kermit survive the karate chop are in bed (or should be) and little persons like me are killing time waiting for the grown-up programmes. Come on Beeb, think small.

Lovelaw (BBC 2) was all about boffing. In Japan young people do it warily so as not to upset their parents' traditions. In California they do it with ignorant abandon. Kenyans do it to show off and Indians, bless their little cotton saris, don't do it at all.

In fact, it all sounded like a microcosm of the Home Counties or anywhere else you care to name. Some people boff before laying supine on the nuptial couch and others don't. I was not bowled over by that particular revelation

News at Ten (ITV) showed a Chinese lung cancer sufferer undergoing an operation fully concious while doctors wiggled the acupuncture needles dotting his body. It was impressive - just so long as you weren't eating your supper at the time.

Forty Minutes (BBC 2) fired my dread of ever being locked up. The cameras spent ten days in Holloway Prison mostly watching women in the psychiatric wing, known to other inmates as The Muppet House. It was pure Kafka.

Overcrowded, understaffed and repressive, the prison was at boiling point with women yet to be found guilty. They were sad, not bad, someone said. But they were locked away 23 hours a day. That's sad and bad.

BODY AND SOUL

LIKE sex and politics, religion was often a dinner party topic. John loved to debate but stuck to his agnostic stance. Like many he had a hidden desire to be convinced about God but the logical side of him was too strong.

His mind was always open to ideas, however, and he happily wandered off to a spiritualist meeting but came back unconverted. The Jehovah's Witnesses who foolishly strayed up his front path invariably regretted it as he kept them talking on the doorstep for hours - whatever the weather.

Despite becoming increasingly ill John never took his health seriously and with his irrepressible sense of humour made light of his hospital stays. The final piece in the book was written just six months before he died - in the same ward and still joking till the end.

29 March, 1989

How I've learnt to put God in His place

MY MINIMAL interest in religion received an unexpected upsurge the other day when two Mormons appeared on my doorstep.

Instead of the usual crewcutted, blue-suited young men wearing Latter Day infibulating underpants, I was confronted by two personable and comely wenches.

No matter that they were disciples of Joseph Smith, of Utah Salt Flats notoriety, when you get to my age and pretty girls want to talk to you, then you damned well listen.

At least it made a change from those po-faced adolescents who have witnessed Jehovah and will tell you that Cardinal Heenan has wasted his life studying theology because he is wrong. Out of the mouths of babes and suckers . . .

The point is that none of these doorstep evangelists will accept that religion is largely an accident of geography. For instance, if you live in India it's odds on that someone will come arapping and try to convert you to Hinduism.

If you live in China, you are likely to be besieged by devotees of Confucius, while the Japanese get huge dollops of Shintoism with their boiled rice and sake.

To be an Iranian is to be up to the lower lip in Islamic fundamentalism and to see nothing wrong in stoning women to death for real, imagined or invented adultery, or to seek the murder of an author with whose views you disagree.

To live in Ulster is to be full of hatred, either for the Pope or for William of Orange, and to tote messengers of death in the name of God with peripheral politics as a secondary consideration.

In Beirut, you are either a Christian or a Druze, both creeds carrying a licence to blast the other to death. In Sri Lanka, Tamils have usurped the popularity of clay pigeons.

The world over, Jews are still reviled as much for their religion as for their fabled ability to make money and do well in business. Hitler was able to exploit this myth at a time when most German Jewry was living below the poverty line.

If you really want to be frightened for the future of mankind, listen to a Presbyterian preaching about the false beliefs of Roman Catholics and ridiculing the aims and aspirations of the ecumenical movement. God it's chilling.

You can, if you wish, hark back to Richard Coeur de Lion and his offensive crusades to gain access for Christians to Jerusalem. It seems that the intolerance and cruelty of religion has always been with us - and in the name of God.

Which brings me to the Easter message of David Jenkins, the controversial Bishop of Durham, whose flexing of his intellect frequently gets him into trouble while winning my admiration. The thinking Christian is far preferable to the blind, slavish believer.

Jenkins essayed the notion that the resurrection of Christ was spiritual rather than physical. Not such an alarming idea if you weigh up the odds of someone being certified as dead then rising up to do business as usual.

If you must cling to religion, which is often no more than an emotional crutch to make you feel better about having done wrong, it is as well also to maintain at least a tangential hold on reality.

It is one of the truisms of life that if, via prayer, you talk to God, that is praiseworthy. If, on the other hand, God talks to you, then men in white coats are likely to cart you off to some secure place with a promise of jelly for tea.

It is also a sobering thought that, were Jesus to return to Earth today, the same men would go into action, and a middle-class Tory JP would have no hesitation in incarcerating Him for His own good.

You have only to look at Western civilisation's perception of Christ to see how well-tailored it wants its religion to be. He is always depicted as white, when the likelihood is that He was very dark brown with Semitic features.

Yet, most adherents of the man-made faith of the Church of England would prefer to see him as a Caucasian native of the Home Counties. It is one of the great aberrations that the Establishment worships a Jew while secretly sneering at his descendants.

Now we have the unedifying prospect of Dr Robert Runcie flying to the Vatican City to placate Pope John Paul over the issue of ordaining women. Has that gender suddenly become detached from the human race?

It is surely one of the gigantic absurdities of inflexible religion that, apart from being unable to unite in a common cause which espouses love, charity, understanding and the turning of the other cheek, it should be guilty of the most blatant act of discrimination.

The Church, of whatever denomination, is as male-orientated as any exclusive club for "gentlemen." And, as we know, there is many a Christian golfer who puts above the Ten Commandments the unwritten law: Thou shalt not tee off with a Jew or a black.

Pretty Mormons aside, I think shall remain within the ranks of committed agnostics. On the whole they seem to be much nicer, more tolerant folk who have no prejudices in their heads and no murder in their hearts.

And we may all agree that there's not much wrong with religion that could not be solved by the elimination of pure, unabashed bigotry.

20 May, 1988

Back in the old routine

IT'S maddening. Just when I've reached the age with allows me to go to the bathroom unaccompanied, now I have to yelp for help in pulling on a pair of socks. It makes me feel like a big girl's blouse.

If, indeed, God had anything to do with the creation of my miserable body it must have been on a wet Monday morning, or maybe a Friday afternoon when he was in a hurry to zip off to Eden for a spot of gardening. Nothing basically wrong with his genetic engineering, but the exterior finish was dodgy.

He made a mare's nest of the features, was niggardly with the hair and definitely skimped on the legs. I could live with all that, if only he'd given me a reliable back. Who wants to look like a Greek god if you can't even win a tussle with your boxer shorts?

The other morning I aimed a foot at a leghole and the little devil who inhabits my lumbar region got out his pincers and gave my spine a malicious squeeze. The scream was followed by an undignified crash to the floor and the utterance of an extremely short word born of anger and frustration.

Displaying really touching sensitivity, my wife said she would have me committed to a home for incurable cussers. There followed an exchange which, later that day, cost me a small fortune in narcissi and irises. Falling over in agony can be expensive.

Unless you are really addicted to denting the bedroom floor, it can also be a bit of a nuisance. Everything, including the WC, seems a world away when you are temporarily paralysed in the supine position. Or even when standing erect. To move an inch is to risk a spasm of lacerating pain.

My former GP watched me hobble into his surgery on a walking stick and came up with a brilliant remedy. "Go and sit in a bath as hot as you can bear it," he said. Pushing back the frontiers of medical science, I emerged from the tub a different man. Now I looked like a wrinkled prune with terrible backache.

You can, of course, be put into traction. This involves having your legs hoisted in the air (not a pretty sight) while someone dangles a JCB from each foot. I know a few sufferers who left hospital uncured, but with the additional bonus of sore ankles.

For extreme cases, depending on the cause, there is an operation. Techniques must have advanced since my trouble began 26 years ago, but then it was considered a dicey business. There were horror stories about patients who ended up worse off. I would never risk it.

You learn to live with it, except that when it gets really bad I can always go to that nice man in Woolton who pummels me and seems to wrap my little limbs around my neck. When he unwraps them, I can walk upright again and the problem disappears for months.

He is a chiropractor, one of a breed of body manipulators thick on the ground in North America but not so profuse in Britain. For years the medical profession scorned them as quacks and carried on dispensing surefire prescriptions for hot baths and painkillers.

Swimmer David Wilkie won his Olympic Gold with the aid of chiropractic, Don Revie employed it when he was England team manager, Cleo Laine and Jenny Lee-Smith, European golf champion, are happy to endorse it. So is Roger Utley, the England rugby team coach, and countless other sporting types.

There is the documented case of a woman who spent five months on her back with hospital treatment and could walk only with the aid of elbow crutches and a steel corset. After two visits to a chiropractor she could walk unaided.

It doesn't work for everyone, because there are so many things that can go wrong with a back. Jane Fonda might yet regret all those frenetic aerobics and ask for aid to don her hose. Hopefully there might be twinges in store for those bores who jog everywhere and sneer at my figure.

A couple of years ago a lecturer at Liverpool Polytechnic began a research project into back strain. Perhaps jokingly, he advised couples intent on coupling to first limber up. There are times when if I get one leg into bed I'm verging on a state of ecstasy.

Another researcher in Manchester believes he might be on the way to finding a cure for chronic sufferers with a drug which could correct the enzyme deficiency which prevents the healing agent from dispersing properly. It's a nice theory and hope it works.

Mostly, I can stand the pain, but the humiliation is unbearable. One morning I rose and, totally naked, was frozen to the spot. Bellowing down the stairs for help brought only this response: "Don't worry, son. Mummy's coming to dress you now." She could hardly be smacked when I needed to lean on her.

On another occasion, I sort of fell over in Wrexham and had to sit on the kerb for 20 minutes. It was so embarrassing as people walked around me and thought the worst. "No, I'm not daft or drunk," I wanted to shout. Not that anyone seemed the least bit interested in my plight.

There was also the time when I had to be carried out of a Cardiff office in the chair on which I had been sitting working all night. Back pain is not funny - except to those who make coarse allegations about what you might have been up to the previous night.

I know from ominous twinges that it will soon be time to have another pummelling and some artistic leg swinging. Then, at least, I shall be able to put on a pair of socks by myself.

3 November, 1987

A bloom with a clue to the hereafter

NOT BLESSED with a figure which attracts wolf whistles or coarse suggestions - not even from undiscriminating stokers - I did feel something of a great jessie walking through Wallasey carrying a single long-stemmed chrysanthemum.

To the denim-clad youths who shot me some very suspicious sidewise glances, this must have been a sight akin to Big Daddy wearing a satin bow in his hair.

But what cared I for their ignorance? One was so dumb he could not distinguish my bloom from a pansy, a word which drifted across the street as I boldly strode out with head carried only marginally higher than navel.

They could not know that I was en route to another world from which the dear departed would send messages of comfort to those still on "this side". This they would do through petals pressed to the forehead of a medium called Edward Grenyer.

Since British Telecom, for all its sophisticated equipment, has difficulty in relaying local communiques, this horticultural hot-line to the living dead seemed to merit scrutiny.

So it was that I turned up at Wallasey Spiritualist Church with 39 others bearing posies and freshly garnered cuttings from their gardens. We paid £1.50 each, had our offerings tagged with cloakroom tickets and laid them on a table beneath the stage.

Soothing music insinuated itself from a tape recorder while a woman bustled about trying to flog raffle tickets for a donkey (a stuffed toy very much of this world) standing uneasily atop the piano.

The audience awaiting Mr Grenyer's demonstration of "flower sentience" was composed mainly of women - 97 per cent I would gauge. Perhaps they were hoping for more response from the victims of rigor mortis than those with whom they live in monosyllabic matrimony.

We were a Heinz 57 bunch. I was flanked by a middle-aged man whose contours suggested a rigid diet of beer and chips and by a young wench whose hair-do might well have concealed a gang of avian squatters.

Mr Grenyer, a bit of a smoothie, began with a long-winded prayer calling for the Maker's blessing on all creatures great and small. The list bordered on the interminable, stopping just short of begging benedictions for tarantulas and the tsetse fly.

Then it was time for a spot of sentience which, he told us, was unlikely to happen unless we believed, created our own power and sent fields of energy surging up the stems. Being incapable of a decent surge these days, I was not surprised the spirits gave my chrysanth the elbow.

But a rose picked up Henry who, in life, apparently had a metal plate in his skull. Perhaps it was this which brought his message to an abrupt end there and then, but "a coloured gent" stepped in to send his regards.

There was a divorce in the offing, two rings and a watch of significance, someone called Agnes and a man who while on "this side" often had to be prised out of his favourite Fair Isle pullover. The recipient of all this fragmented information said she understood perfectly.

Mr Grenyer then declared himself to be excited, having "got the nod" from a lady with a bad back. Adopting her persona he said, "Why don't you shut your mouth?" This, seemingly, was a reference to a young man full of himself who is soon to cop a parking ticket.

There was a dog called Zebedee, someone who had voice box trouble and a meaningful brooch. Indeed, there was hardly a message which did not include painful ailments and items of jewellery.

Next on the line was "Tiger," a gent with a fondness for whippets and rabbits. Aunt Clara and Margaret made an appearance along with a bag of pear drops. Again, through another persona, Mr Grenyer asked, "Who's got housemaid's knee?"

Whoever the sufferer, he or she was luckier than others in the message who were afflicted by stomach cancer, neuralgia and a hiatus hernia. The pear drops apart, "Tiger" was not the bearer of good news.

Mr Grenyer then took a message for someone in the audience whom he was sure was a medium and was going to eliminate chips from her diet. She would, though, remain fond of Angel Delight. Her aura came through very strongly. If she were not a medium, then she was definitely spiritually sensitive.

All this turned out to be a massive clanger dropped on "the other side". The woman concerned said the information was entirely without meaning. She denied having caused a crossed line by letting anyone else handle her flower.

He ploughed on with another message which was understood, although all the names cited had no significance whatsoever. It was soon after this that the medium's flower power wilted, leaving 31 blooms with not a word to impart. I was sentient to the need to visit the loo.

Through its door I heard a woman complaining bitterly that she and her friends had between them parted with £7.50 and had heard not a peep from their posies. A man told her they could never guarantee a message for everyone. When the energy dried up, there was nothing to be done.

"Well, it's made me even more of a septic (sic)," she said.

My own feeling was that, her money apart, she had missed very little. The information which came over was mostly useless and the few positive messages which came through were confined to such pithy phrases as, "Keep going, our Kid." There is little comfort to be derived from a dish of Angel Delight, a bag of pear drops or a Fair Isle pullover in dire need of a good wash.

When it comes to flower sentience, I think these gullible ladies would have learned far more from Gardeners' Question Time.

14 January, 1987

Old habits and even old bangers die gasping

MY DOCTOR, an Egyptian of infinite charm and a walking, talking credit to the Hippocratic Oath, wants me to renounce both tobacco and alcohol. "You must change your habits," he told me rather sternly.

I know him well enough to have replied: "I think I'd rather change my doctor." It was a poor joke to which he responded with a smile chillier than this week's frosts. It suggested he might well like to change his patient.

Who can blame him? Why minister to a body engine that refuses to be regularly serviced and desperately needs a de-coke? He is a mechanic tending an old banger which only just scrapes through its MOT.

Victor, as I like to think of him, radiates good health and oozes common sense from every pore. Without ever having flirted with the weed himself, he understands what it is to be hooked.

Once, when my wife sneaked on me, he counselled her to be tolerant, to grasp the concept of addiction and to embrace the philosophy of mercy and compassion. I never knew that compassion could be equated with the Spanish Inquisition.

And it became definitely subversive. What can you say when a four-year-old child wags a rigid index finger in your ravaged face and says: "I suppose you know you're killing yourself." You feel dirty, weak and irresponsible.

Unfortunately, if you have been dirty, weak and irresponsible since the age of 15, it is very difficult to become clean, strong and upright in your forties. Old habits, even repulsive ones, die hard.

My family and Victor want me to die easily at a good age. Too many people dear to me, including one this week, have painfully caved in to the cruel erosions of lung cancer.

Yet, during the effort of concentration needed to produce this inconsequential souffé, I will have consumed the better part of a whole pack. It's madness, particularly since I am mentally prepared for the ordeal of attending today's funeral of a man I revered.

Not that I haven't tried to pare down the obscene profits of the tobacco barons. There have been several attempts at denial through sheer will-power. I have to say that will's batteries were quite simply knackered.

Then I forked out £6 for a packet of therapeutic chewing gum prescribed by Victor. I can heartily recommend these little lozenges to anyone whose taste-buds are dead and buried or who has an insatiable craving for Polyfilla.

With a colleague, I attended a hypnotherapy clinic at which we watched soothing video-taped pastoral scenes and listened to a velvet voice congratulating us on having kicked the habit. The tape ended with an exhortation for us to carry a packet of unopened fags. Whenever we felt the need to smoke we were meant to give it a stony stare and say: "I am your master and I have beaten you."

We had negotiated only 75 yards of Bold Street when my mate produced his pack and said: "OK pal, you are my master and you have bloody well beaten me." It wasn't long before I followed suit.

I had another friend who, on his way home from a pub, stopped the car and impulsively threw his cigarettes and lighter over a hedge. To give him his due, he waited until dawn before scouring the fields for his lost possessions.

Then I went to see a lovely lady called Sue Washington, who put me in a reclining chair and talked softly while, through closed eyes, I saw images of soaring birds silhouetted against a blood-orange sun. I was so relaxed my head nearly fell off.

My consumption of cancerettes over the next few days fell by 90 per cent. Unfortunately, before my next booster session Sue was taken ill and it was a fortnight before we met again. In that short time the magic had worn off.

The birds were grounded and the demonic nicotine coursing through my blood was demanding to be fed as never before. My chest was protesting with sounds reminiscent of a geriatric chapel organ. I hated the music, but subserviently danced to its tune.

My dictionary defines nicotine as a poisonous alkaloid derived from tobacco leaves. Presumably those MPs who lobby so assiduously for the tobacco industry use greatly different works of reference - such as cash registers and pocket calculators.

Successive Chancellors of the Exchequer have tried to preserve our health with swingeing increases in tobacco taxes - then, like Fagin, rubbed their hands with glee at having picked more than a pocket or two. The hypocrites.

They are only marginally better than those who manufacture the evil tubes, and far more cynical than those of us daft enough to have taken the first few potentially fatal drags that made us addicts.

We can blame no one but ourselves. Perhaps this morning, as the wasted body of Ron Hills is cremated, I will finally find a cure. I hope so.

30 November, 1988

Amazing grace ... but not for hedonistic me

THERE IS something remorselessly depressing and inevitable about the start of the working week. You could build a breeze-block wall around your bed and Mondays would still nastily insinuate themselves beneath your coverlet, no matter how heavy its tog-rating.

It was in this hilarious frame of mind that I emptied the porch of its menacing mail, only to have one blurred eye arrested by a message from Bishop J.C. Ryle. He must have written it in a darkened room while enduring a pernicious bout of migraine.

This eminent cleric is, obviously a bit of a wag, although evidently sincere. Heavily committed to the assumption that I shall eventually die (do the immortal ever pop their clogs?) he promised me eternal misery with a load of indignation and wrath as some kind of bonus.

Dwelling upon the thought that you simply cannot beat a good laugh on a wet Monday morning, I turned to the accompanying mailing-shot. It offered me a chance to be saved by the Free Presbyterian Church's Old Time Gospel Campaign to be held in Wallasey's Welsh Presbyterian Church (Kindly Granted).

This is not the ideal way for the avowedly hedonistic to spend an evening, but who could pass up the chance of special singing and testimonies en route to an eternity free of gloom and fuel bills? Well, most of Wallasey it seems.

I made a poor start. Drawn to a room bubbling with cheerful noise I opened the door to find myself the centre of amazed attention by a horde of Girl Guides. Wrong church - but I was soon on the path to righteousness, if by the wrong door. To the tune of "Amazing Grace" I passed right in front of the preacher, the Rev. Hillis Fleming, of Liverpool.

The room was crammed to underflowing. There were 26 of us if you counted the baby, mostly women of advanced age with a collective penchant for berets and knitted hats. The pianist was more dashing in a parrot-green trilby and enthusiastically sprang to her instrument whenever a hymn was announced.

The place was festooned with brightly coloured posters whose words, rather like those of the hymns, encouragingly promised doom and unrivalled privation for snivelling wretches who didn't toe the line.

After a woman with a bell in nearly every tooth had sung a solo, Mrs Fleming was called forward to give testimony. As if to prove that their church is not entirely devoid of humour, Mr Fleming said it was one of few occasions when he could tell her to be brief. There were some who nearly laughed.

After relating her quest for a meeting with God, she told how she was directed towards the Free Presbyterians "to be separated from the ecumenical movement, the World Council of Churches and the Roman Catholics with their false teachings." The Almighty must have been toying with religious apartheid on that particular day.

Rather predictably the minister, who bore an uncanny resemblance to Sunny Jim Callaghan, elected to sermonise on sin or, as he put it, "all Hell let loose".

Then, with a commendable show of unabashed candour, Mr Fleming confessed to having a police record. My trembling pen was poised. It seems that about 40 years ago tearaway cyclist Hillis had coughed to the missing rear light job. He had escaped a stretch in the joint by paying out eleven shillings in fines and costs.

Hardly in the Kray mould, but it had given him a record which the police could call up today. Patent rubbish, of course, but it led to his analogy of all transgressions being logged by the Deity. Already I was becoming restive.

However, the amazing Sunny Fleming soon made me sit up with one of his more contentious revelations. The reason people didn't like talking about cancer was because they knew it was the result of sin, he said. All terrible diseases were the result of sin.

To be fair, the mailing-shot had specified "old time" gospel, but had said nothing about its positively antediluvian delivery by a partially-sighted dinosaur.

Best of all, I liked the fable about the beautiful swan spotting a pig having some fun in a mud-hole. The bird alighted on a green tor and invited the hog to join it in a beautiful place. Porky asked if there were any mud-holes up there and, receiving a reply in the negative, elected to stay where it was.

Mr Fleming was triumphant. That story characterised sinners, he said. They found their own pile of muck and were content to roll around in it.

There was no mention of the poverty or other dire straits which might have driven them there in the first place.

Neither do I recall any reference to enlightened Christian understanding on the frailties of homo sapiens. Just loads of inflexible unyielding cant promising the worst of everything to those not made of Mr Fleming's deluxe three-ply moral fibre.

I end on a note of hope. The baby unfailingly chuckled after each purse-lipped pronouncement. At least someone there had some sense.

1 October, 1986

Pants, with a pinch of salt

I AM NOT normally given to asking young men with what type of nether garments they gird their loins. Not in a first encounter, anyway. One's motives could be regarded with deep suspicion and, more importantly, could earn one a nasty smack in the mouth.

However, it was with a boldness born of sheer nosiness that I recently found myself quizzing two fresh-faced youths about their underpants. Rude of me, I suppose, but they shouldn't have interrupted my Saturday brunch to advance the arrogant notion that I was steering the wrong path through life.

Looking through the glazed front door I knew instantly from whence they came - a far-off place in which all the tailors mass-produce neat blue suits and in which the barbers specialise in the drastic style of the sheep shearer.

They were Mormon missionaries who, rather like the Chinese, all tend to look the same.

I was racking my brains for the biblical equivalent of "Get lost" when I suddenly recalled having read a magazine article about the Salt Lake City slickers. There was an intriguing reference to what still remains to me the secret world beneath their trousers.

It seems that unmarried lads are kitted out with underwear cunningly (and cruelly) designed to suppress lust and keep Percy Filth at bay. Now if you think about it - and I know you already are - the concept of a male chastity belt built into a chap's knickers is quite stunning. How do they do it?

Or is the garment itself the modern version of the mediaeval infibulator? If they, or it, are strong enough to repulse Percy, doesn't it make for gross inconvenience in the convenience? Are they so tight that no blood ever flows beyond the knee cap and do they have to have a padlock removed at bedtime?

How complex a design that could restrain a really determined Latter Day Saint from being a bit of a devil with the dames.

These and other Mittyesque considerations had occupied my wandering mind for a good hour one rainy afternoon. Now more absurd images were popping up as the earnest acolytes launched into their spiel about Joseph Smith's vision. Here was my chance to unlock the secret of the sealed panties.

Tongue only slightly in cheek I inquired if, apart from giving birth to a sect, Joe had also dreamed up the device which stopped others giving birth to anything at all. And anyway, I pressed them, how on earth did it work? My interest was serious.

Had I been a rookie dentist I could not have hit a rawer nerve. The younger elder, aged about 19, flushed with evident anger and curtly told me that if I wanted to know anything about his underpants I would have to join the church. It seemed too high a price to pay just because they are not readily available in Marks and Spencer.

I apologised for my impertinence, but they were already on their way and clearly convinced they had encountered a lingerie fetishist. On the plus side, my fried egg had still not set hard enough to be used as a frisbee and I had found a sure-fire way of ridding my doorstep of persistent Mormons.

This is a matter for rejoicing. These days, it seems, the world and his wife beat a path to your door. One's house is no longer one's castle because so many invaders keep forcing you to raise the portcullis. Domestic peace and privacy are now as rare as hamburger stands alongside the Wailing Wall.

Jehovah's Witnesses are just as troublesome as the other lot and equally convinced that anyone outside their ranks is a misguided heathen who has yet to discover The Truth. I've tried shouting "blood transfusion" at them but they always produce religious tracts which conclusively prove I am related to Dracula.

Witnesses are invariably accompanied by wan children and teenagers, presumably tagging along as apprentices in the art of conversion. What is frightening is the conviction with which they tell you that noted theologians are barking up the wrong tree. From the mouths of indoctrinated babes and sucklings.

And it's no good pointing out that they have no business to be ringing your doorbell when they should have disappeared from the face of the earth some year's back, when the rest of us miraculously survived their confidently predicted Armageddon. They have an answer for everything and I cannot resist an argument.

But then, I haven't seen the JWs for a while. With luck, the word will have spread that the peculiar bloke at No. 24 keeps them talking for ages, even when its freezing, and mixes theological debate with cryptic references to "another wasted egg."

Evenings are reserved for the peddlers of loft insulation, fitted kitchens, double glazing, brushes, sponges, dusters, and that dreadful stone cladding with which some neighbours deface their homes and, consequently, the street. There are raffle ticket sellers and collectors for this cause and that.

Dubious looking men ask for old furniture and brass, hoping to con you out something worth a small fortune for which you paid a few quid years ago. Others ask if you have any old clothes. I always reply, "Yes, and it would be inconvenient to take them off right now."

The porch is ankle-deep in unsolicited mailing shots and free newspapers. Businessmen trying to weather the recession employ tele-sales girls to ring you up in the middle of dinner. Between the noise from the door and the phone, there are days when I wander around like Quasimodo cursing the bells.

Like Garbo, I want to be left alone. I wonder if she'll put me up for a few days. She could probably do with a bit of company.

21 March, 1990

A hard day's night down in Ward 33

JUST A FEW yards down the corridor of Ward 33 lay Idwal, bald-pated, side hair hanging to his jowels in curtain fashion and naked bulbous belly looking like an ungilded dome that had slipped off the Kremlin roof.

He was the image of the world's naughtiest Troll in repose, except that his peace, and ours, would soon be rent asunder by The Cough - featured nightly at approximately 11.45 with admission unavoidable.

It began with a loud grumble in the diaphragm, then crawled on to painfully negotiate the fissured causeways of what were probably once a perfectly good pair of lungs. It sounded as if someone had drawn a wire brush across the inner wall of his chest.

After a fractious skirmish with the rough terrain of the throat, the guttural left-overs of a tiring spasm had Idwal reaching for his oxygen mask to await the next encounter. We also waited, wondering if it was worth trying to nod off.

To my left in Bay 12a was Bob, blissfully out of touch with reality, singing softly throughout the night, frantically chafing his hands together or else rattling the bars which were meant to stop him rolling out of bed.

Now he had wet himself yet again and Tony Higgins, a young Glaswegian, and another nurse came to change the sheets and the soaking night-shirt. Bob, with the musculature of Ghandi sat in a chair and asked, "Whose birthday is it anyway? I've got lots of acker on me cracker."

To my right was a man who punctuated rare silences with bouts of wind-breaking almost rhythmic enough to be of interest to some avant garde librettist. He never excused himself nor apologised.

We all detested him, not least because of his imperious attitude toward the staff and a lack of basic manners which would have precluded any one of our number taking him to the bin.

The bed opposite mine was empty. Its former occupant had died just ten minutes after my arrival. Old Bob was now castigating someone in quite foul language and I just knew it was going to be a long night.

In fact, they all were. The days, too, were interminable and jokes about forming an escape committee and auditioning for the John Mills role soon palled. So, in truth, did our enforced togetherness and friction was inevitable.

With only six patients to each bay, familiarity bred its usual progeny and a flare-up over politics led to two sexagenarian heart attack victims talking of exchanging blows. In fact, either could have been beaten by a custard tart in their state of health.

One was a likeable Roman Catholic who gave me instruction. "No two ways about it, lad. The quickest way to get a man down is to go for the balls." It was no surprise to learn he had been both a seafarer and a publican.

Given his demeanour, the other should have been on a women's ward comparing symptoms, drugs, side-effects and water retention. He wandered into other bays and spent hours dispensing advice to the less knowledgeable.

I really took a shine to him when he said, "I know why the Welsh keep a welcome in the hillsides. It's because they don't want us in the towns." He cackled as if he had said something funny.

He then launched into a comically misinformed dissertation on arsonists, based on the belief that anyone on the wrong side of Offa's Dyke is born carrying a box of Swan Vesta and a pop bottle full of petrol.

You need to live with someone like that for a few days to realise how provocative immunity to reason and common sense makes them. Since he wouldn't, or couldn't, listen, I simply promised to set fire to him at the earliest opportunity.

One of the lighter moments of my stay at Arrowe Park was when an obviously nervous young nurse approached my bed and drew the curtains. I asked what she intended doing and she said she was there to measure my leg.

"Just put down that it's as embarrassingly short as it was yesterday. In fact, no change," I said. She exhorted me not to mess around and I had to tell her that she had misheard the instructions and should be straining her tape around my abdomen.

There was alarm and excitement when another nurse pulled up my pyjama jacket and aimed a hypodermic at my stomach. "What the hell's this for?" I barked. "Now come along, Mr Hill, you know you have this done every night," she said patiently.

It was left to my fellow inmates, between gusts of laughter, to point out the cardboard name plate at the head of my bed. Such moments of mild drama become major talking points at close quarters.

Down the corridor in a room of his own was a man we held in some awe. He had lost both legs above the knee and, even by the generous standards of the staff, was given almost limitless licence to be awkward.

One night, after an ill-tempered bout of buzzing his personal alarm he shouted and swore at everyone in uniform. He allowed them just enough time to return to their station before buzzing again.

The nurses sighed, some swore quietly, but their smiles were soon back in place. Part of their job is to know when cries of anger mask fear and frustration, when a man is really bemoaning the terrible knowledge that he will never be the same again.

Bob carried on singing. Idwal, and those like him, all but coughed up their hearts and men with deathly pallors wept silently for an uncertain future. The angels smiled on and worked through just another night of life and death on Ward 33.